REKINDLED

GAME OF LOVE SERIES

SUSAN SCOTT SHELLEY

CHAPTER ONE

Gemma Norwood shivered in her sweatshirt and glanced at the lake. The winter wind whipped blasts of icy cold air in stinging, tingling shots. Four years of living in Los Angeles had softened her tolerance of the harsh New York winter in the Catskill Mountains. Snow-dusted pine trees and calm waters set up a picture-perfect backdrop to the excited chatter and colorful bathing suits of the dozens and dozens of people milling around the embankment.

Beside her, Jocelyn pointed a gloved finger to the snow covering parts of the ground and gave an exaggerated shiver. "What idiot decided that jumping into a lake at the end of January would be a smart idea?"

"Well, actually, you did." She laughed and dodged her best friend's swat. The foreign laugh was something she hadn't experienced in a long time. Life wasn't funny while a career, and a dream, floundered like a fish suffocating on dry land. Twenty-four hours ago, she'd stood staring at palm trees, wondering if she'd ever see the West Coast again. Hopefully, a dip in the nearly frozen water would shock an answer into her system.

Murmuring about hypothermia and frostbitten toes, Jocelyn stamped her fur-lined boots against the ground. "My dad and brother decided this would be a good thing. If it were up to me, we'd hold a bake sale instead."

Gemma sidestepped two little girls twirling in circles, giggling over the chance to wear their bathing suits in the middle of winter. "Your charity will raise a lot of money this way."

"I'm thrilled about that part, but I'll leave the jumping in the lake part to you crazy people. I'll stick with my duties of organizing the event, helping out with pre-plunge participant check-in, and handing out hot drinks at the refreshment stand after the plunge."

"I'm happy to help you pass out the hot chocolate."

Amid banners promoting Hudson Contractors' Caring Home Repair Fund, people were jumping around in creative attempts to keep warm. But there weren't any signs of Mr. Hudson or his first-born son.

"Are your dad and brother here?" Straining to keep her voice casual, she peeled her sweatshirt over her head. Goosebumps seemed to pop out on top of goosebumps. The warm temperatures of LA had never seemed so far away.

"Dad's probably checking to see if the mic's working for his speech. He's bummed about not jumping in the water this year. The cold weather is too hard on him." Jocelyn's smile dimmed. "Ever since his heart attack, he just doesn't have the same stamina."

The heart attack and triple bypass surgery that followed had taken a toll on Jocelyn's entire family.

Gemma squeezed her hand. From three thousand miles away, she hadn't been able to offer more than prayers and a sympathetic ear. "What about your brother?"

In the whirlwind rush of packing her bags and arranging for the dog's travel and flying home to Hunter's Peak, she deliberately hadn't asked Jocelyn about Adam, preferring to put off the conversation for as long as possible. A decision she now regretted. If he showed up, she'd have to rely on her acting skills to help her get through the encounter.

"Adam is supposed to be here, but I don't see him. You know, I just realized something. The first time we held the plunge was the first time you two met." Jocelyn's voice took on the extra-cheerful tone she always used when talking to Gemma about Adam. Being her ex-boyfriend's sister could have meant an awkward end to their friendship, but Jocelyn seemed just as determined as Gemma to maintain their relationship. And when she occasionally hinted at trying to get them back together, Gemma ignored her and changed the subject.

"It doesn't matter. I'm doing this for me. Not anyone else." Her hands shook as she shimmied out of her yoga pants. She dreaded seeing Adam now that she'd reached her lowest point. Her stomach clenched, and she searched the crowd. No sign of him. A deep breath eased her nerves.

Jocelyn glanced at her and shivered. "This isn't exactly the welcome home I'd choose, but to each her own."

She needed to do it. Maybe it was stupid. Maybe she would regret it. But maybe, just maybe, she'd get her wish and figure out what to do next.

She handed the shirt and pants to Jocelyn, and they

slowly shuffled into the crowd of people waiting for the Polar Plunge to begin.

"Do you think someone will recognize you and ask for an autograph?" Cradling the clothes and a few towels, Jocelyn tugged her hat tighter onto her head.

"I doubt it." Four years of landing bit parts in B-movies didn't translate into a large fan base. Heck, it hardly translated into any fan base. And while four years of catering countless parties had improved her culinary skills and paid the bills, it didn't guarantee loyalty.

Frosty chaos? Yeah, that was her life for the past three days. A job lost. A rejection from the last production company she could find. Both had dumped a bucket of icy water onto her acting dream and thrown her into a tailspin. Admitting her exhaustion, frustration, and fear to her parents resulted in a plane ticket home. They didn't care if she had her name in bright lights, but she sure did.

Jocelyn's dad, wearing a Hudson Contractors jacket, stepped onto a wooden platform on the shore. The crowd's noise lowered to murmurs as he gave a speech about the charity. When he finished, Jocelyn nudged Gemma's arm. "I'll wait for you by the fence near the parking lot. Don't turn into an icicle out there."

An air horn blared. The crowd surged and swept Gemma to the water's edge. She forged ahead, splashing into the lake. Frigid water slapped her skin. Some enterprising soul dove into the water headfirst. His belly flop sent a swell of water over Gemma's chest and chin.

Sucking in a breath, she stiffened her muscles. She had known it would be cold, but she wasn't prepared for the frigid temperature. She should have been. She'd done this before. But back then, she'd had Adam's hand to hold. And being in love with him made the entire world seem warmer, safer, more comfortable.

But that ended when he boarded a plane bound for major-league baseball in Northern California and left her behind.

Teeth chattering, body shaking, she fought the bone-numbing chill seizing her system. The stark cold was a sharp reminder of her lonely reality. All around her, people grabbed onto each other. Shrieks and screams accompanied laughter. Someone shouted an idea to swim across the lake. The couple next to her shook their heads and headed back to shore. Chill turned to an ache. Her toes hurt, her legs hurt, but she kept moving, determined to stay in the water just a little longer.

When the water level reached her chest, she turned back. Her foot slipped on a rock, and she pitched forward. Water rose up to meet her and closed over her head. It flowed into her nose and into her mouth. The shock of cold seized her muscles. She sank further. Heart pounding, she kicked out and felt for the lake floor. She pushed up and broke the surface, sputtering and coughing.

A large hand curled around her elbow. "Are you all right?"

The rough gravel of his voice, sharp and sexy, pumped fresh adrenaline into her system. Continuing to cough, she regained her balance and looked up the muscled torso and into the face of Adam Hudson. His firm mouth, straight nose, and intense brown eyes were just as she'd remembered.

The small scar running through his left eyebrow hadn't been there before. He'd earned the mark eight months ago, but not being a part of his life meant she didn't have the right to check up on him.

News of Adam Hudson, starting pitcher for the Sacramento Storm, getting hit by a line-drive that fractured his skull, had made national news and scared her enough to drive six hours up I-5 North to see him for herself. Heavily medicated, he hadn't known she was there. And the cool blonde who slipped into the room after Gemma had stepped out, solidified the notion that Adam had moved on. In the months that followed, the only way she'd been able to keep informed of his recovery had been phone calls with Jocelyn or scouring sports news sites.

His brows lifted, and his fingers loosened and then tightened their hold. "Gemma."

The surprise in his voice cut through her discomfort. They stood in the crowded water, staring at each other. A rush of memories crashed into her like a tidal wave. Emotions jumbled together—longing, regret, wanting, need.

"Are you hurt?" He stooped, and his gaze searched her face. His other hand gently tapped against her back.

"I'm okay." She stammered through trembling lips and coughed a few more times. Why did he have to find her at such a disadvantage? So much for her plan to appear cool and collected if they met.

"What are you doing here?"

"F-f-f-freezing." Attempting a smile was difficult when frozen cheeks and frozen lips wouldn't cooperate.

Something passed over Adam's features, too quickly for her to name it. "Your lips are blue. Come on, mermaid, time to get out of the water." His hand gripped hers, and he led her through the crowded water to the shore.

Feet like blocks of ice couldn't feel the lake floor. She curled her hand more securely in his and followed his lead, saying a silent prayer that she wouldn't slip under again.

When they reached dry land, his grip remained firm around her fingers. "Where's your towel?"

"Jocelyn's holding my stuff." Her arms trembled. Shaking fingers formed fists in a useless attempt to keep warm. "She was supposed to wait for me by the fence, but I don't see her."

People darted around them, scrambling into dry clothes while a few brave souls ventured back into the icy waters. Gemma pulled her arms in close to her body. She'd forgotten how painful the cold could be.

"You can use mine. Come on." He pulled her through the throng and over to a grassy patch of land spotlighted by sunlight. After rummaging in his gym bag, he handed her a towel. "My sister didn't tell me you were in town."

"I arrived last night."

"I thought your parents were in Florida this time of year."

"They are."

For a moment, they locked eyes and the chaos and noise surrounding them faded. He didn't smile, just watched her with a neutral expression. "They usually have someone rent their house when they're away."

She nodded and wrapped the towel around her waist. Was he happy to see her? Angry? Anything? "I'm staying with Jocelyn."

His mouth hardened into a firm line. "How long are you staying?"

"I haven't decided." Clutching the towel tighter, she

took a step back and drew in a deep breath to ease the tightness in her chest.

Goosebumps dotted his skin. "Let's get you dry, and then some hot chocolate. You'll warm up."

"What about you? Your lips are blue, too."

"I'll be fine." He rubbed his hand through thick, dark brown hair, dripping rivulets of water down his skin. His response echoed their last conversation, when they'd ended their relationship. If he remembered it, he didn't let on. Instead, he pulled another towel from his bag and draped it over her shoulders. "I'll look for my sister. Wait here."

Gemma watched Adam stride into the crowd and rubbed the towel over her skin. The shock of the water was nothing compared to the shock of seeing him again. In all the ways she imagined they'd meet, a sputtering half-rescue in an icy lake hadn't made the list. But he'd been more than civil, he'd been kind. Maybe they could end up being friends.

The hollow feeling in her gut eased but didn't disappear. Being this close to him again only reinforced how much she'd missed him over the last four years.

She wrapped the towel more securely around her body and stamped her feet and wiggled her toes, willing warmth to return. Workout clothes hung out of his open gym bag. She longed to pull on the socks and sweats.

Within a few minutes, Jocelyn and Adam strode toward her. Heat glittered in Adam's eyes. A smile beamed across Jocelyn's face. With a flourish, she held out Gemma's clothes. "Sorry, I was helping set up the refreshments."

Gemma tugged her sweatshirt over her torso, then wriggled out of her bikini top. With her towel wrapped around her waist, taking off the bottoms was nearly impossible, but she managed to slip them off and shimmy into her pants and sneakers without giving anyone a glimpse of something they shouldn't see.

"No coat?" Adam stood in front of her, dressed in sweats and a jacket. His fingers brushed hers when she handed him the towels.

She shrugged and pretended the barb of heat hadn't jolted her senses. "I gave away a lot of stuff before I moved to LA. I didn't anticipate needing a wool coat anymore."

His gaze fixed on her chest and a muscle in his jaw jumped. "You kept my shirt."

She glanced at the scarlet logo of his minor league baseball team emblazoned across the fabric. Heat flooded her cheeks. Keeping his sweatshirt after the breakup was one thing, but now he knew that she'd kept it. No way would she mention how many times she'd worn it or slept in it over the last four years. Why, why, why, did she have to wear it today?

What could she say? Before she could open her mouth, Adam unzipped his coat and placed it over her shoulders. "Here."

She shook her head. "I can't take your jacket."

"Wear it. You're still shivering." His mouth finally lifted into a half smile. "Don't fight me, or I'll sic Jocelyn on you."

"Just wear it, Gem. Adam's tolerance of the cold is as tough as his head is hard. Let's get some hot chocolate. I have to run back to help serve, so I'll see you there." Jocelyn turned away and broke into a jog.

Gemma gripped the coat against her body and turned to Adam. Warmth seeped into her system. "Thanks."

People swarmed around them. He gestured in the direction his sister had ran. "Let's get there before they run out."

Walking side by side brought back a rush of memories of their first meeting at the plunge. She glanced sideways at Adam. Was he thinking about that, too?

Two little boys cut in front of her. She stopped short, and Adam's arm jerked out, blocking her from impact. His arm grazed her shoulder. Barely touching, but she could feel it. His chocolate brown gaze met hers. The spark of electricity that had always crackled between them flared to life so quickly, her breath caught in her lungs.

No. Not now. This wasn't supposed to happen.

Murmuring her thanks, she lowered her gaze and stepped away.

They reached the refreshments. His jacket smelled like him, a familiar mix of soap and cologne. Surrounded by warmth, Gemma gathered her courage. So much needed to be said. When they both had hot chocolate in hand, she faced him. "I'm sorry about your accident."

He lifted his brow and inclined his head. "Thanks. I survived."

"I'm glad you're okay now."

His eyes hardened, and he stared at the lake. "There's a difference between surviving and being okay."

CHAPTER TWO

Damn it. Why had he said that? Wanting to kick himself, Adam glanced at Gemma. Her violet eyes widened, and sympathy, the last thing he wanted to see, appeared across her features.

"What do you mean? You're not okay?" More than sympathy, worry. Her hand touched his forearm. Even through the thick fleece of his shirt, he could feel her touch. Those expressive eyes rounded, and she moved a step closer to his side.

"Forget I said anything." He swallowed the hot chocolate and wished it were a shot of whiskey. No way should he have this conversation with her. No way, not after being apart for so long. No way, but something about Gemma prompted him to open up.

He shook his head. Not happening. He had to solve his problems himself.

After spending eight years in minor league baseball, he'd thought he'd never have a shot at the big league. But the opportunity came, and he'd played so well, the Storm had kept him.

Until his injury.

He resisted the urge to touch his temple and feel for the scar.

Dealing with the after-effects of a concussion and bouts of vertigo was nothing compared to the hellish two months that followed, pitching like a rookie for a minor league club in Reno for his rehab assignment. His pitching accuracy tanked and never recovered. His chance of going back to the Storm faded away.

Stuck in Reno, he wasn't pitching at all by the time his dad had a heart attack on Labor Day. After bouncing around the minors for so long, he didn't want to return to riding buses around the country with eighteen and twenty-year-olds. Asking for a release had made sense. Plus, his family needed him.

"Adam." Water dripped from the ends of Gemma's poker-straight, jet-black hair. Her lush lips pressed together. He could easily remember how they felt moving under his, and how her figure, with just enough curves to make a man beg to see every inch of her body, had molded to his like they were made for each other.

Too many feelings tumbled onto themselves, like a player pile-up after a game. Anger, frustration, longing, regret, and the steady beat of desire that shouldn't still exist. He'd spent every off-season in Hunter's Peak, but as far as he knew, she hadn't come back once since she left for Hollywood. He'd assumed she'd forgotten all about their little town, forgotten all about him. What the hell was she doing here? Why now?

Why now, when he had enough on his mind without adding in a sexy siren whose legs went on for miles, and who left a void in his life that he hadn't been able to fill in the four years they'd been apart.

"It's fine." His cell phone dinged with a missed call alert. He pulled the phone from his bag. The name on the display sent equal parts dread and elation through his system. He'd walked away from baseball, but baseball hadn't forgotten about him. The opportunity to get back into the game had arrived via several teams extending offers for him to show up at spring training. New York, Miami, Philadelphia, and now Boston, all pushing for him to try out for one of their starting pitching jobs.

Pitchers and catchers were due to report to training in the middle of February.

He had three weeks to decide. Three weeks to fix a problem that refused to go away.

He pocketed the phone and faced her. The wind billowed, and her coat flapped open. The familiar logo on her sweatshirt, faded from many washings, distracted him. Why had she kept it?

"I know you asked the team to release you, but I thought that was because your dad got sick. Is your injury still...are you still hurt?" Biting her lip, eyes earnest, she leaned closer. Her hand reached up, as though to touch his face, but she pulled it back to her side and blushed.

Her concern cut into him. On some level, she might still care. He never stopped. "I'm fine."

Faint lines appeared on her forehead, and her stare fixed on his scar. "Really?"

"Really." Pushing aside thoughts of his fall from celebrated major-league starting pitcher to his minor-league rehab assignment disaster, he offered her a smile and changed the subject. "How's Bear doing?"

A dazzling smile spread across her face. "You wouldn't even recognize him now. He's so big."

Soon after they'd adopted the puppy, Adam had received the call he'd waited for since the first time he picked up a baseball. A shot with a major league team. A move that had sent him across the country. A move that had cost him Gemma.

She'd taken off for Hollywood not long after he'd left. Between her acting lessons, auditions, and catering job, and his games, practices, and travel schedule, their relationship fizzled to sporadic phone calls, and then finally, nothing.

He downed the rest of his hot chocolate, but it didn't ease the hollowness in his gut. Neither did a look at the lake. But the dispersing crowd meant time to get to work. A few members of his construction crew milled around, waiting to take down the banners. He waved to catch their attention, nodded for them to begin, and then turned back to Gemma. "I need to help my guys clean up."

Her smile dimmed. "Listen, about what you said earlier…"

The desire to touch her hand or her cheek was so strong, he had to force his hand into his pocket so he wouldn't reach out. "Good seeing you. Take care."

The words sounded so formal, so polite, so not the way he wanted this to end. But his men needed him, and he needed to get away before he made a mistake. One step separated them, then another, and another.

"Wait, you need your jacket." She moved toward him,

and everything in him demanded that he close the rest of the distance.

Resisting the urge shifted his voice into a growl. "Keep it on. Jocelyn will get it back to me later."

Before he did something stupid, like saying he missed her, he walked away.

CHAPTER THREE

After a post-plunge hot shower, Gemma sat at the small table in Jocelyn's kitchen. Steaming bowls of soup warded off the lingering chill. She wrapped a blanket around her shoulders and poured hot tea into two large mugs. Jocelyn's house, a cozy rancher set on the outskirts of town, seemed the perfect quiet place to plan her next move. "Thanks for letting me and this monster crash here."

"Anytime." Jocelyn reached under the table and rubbed Bear's fur. The Akita sat up and laid his paw in her lap. "He's such a good boy."

"He's using his best manners for you," Gemma joked and then turned her head as the tickle in her nose turned into a sneeze.

"I told you jumping into freezing water wasn't smart. You're probably coming down with some weird lake disease." Jocelyn wrinkled her nose and formed her arms into the shape of a cross. "Keep your germs to yourself."

Gemma laughed when Bear's sneeze echoed hers.

"Please. I'm fine. There's too much pepper on my soup, that's all."

The television droned on in the background. Jocelyn switched the channel from a sports network to a popular celebrity gossip show.

Gemma turned away from the screen. "Oh God, please tell me you don't watch those voyeuristic shows. They invent half of their stories and speculate on the rest until the truth is completely skewed."

Except for the occasional party or event, her experience with the paparazzi was limited to her volunteer work at a yearly celebrity-run pet adopt-a-thon. But, she'd seen first-hand how careers and relationships could be ruined by a suggestive photo or a microphone thrust into an actor's face in a heated moment.

Jocelyn shrugged. "I have to watch these shows in case you're ever featured on them. You'd want to know right away, wouldn't you?"

"So, you watch them every day solely for my benefit?"

"Absolutely. What are friends for? It's a burden seeing the all those hot actors, like Tyler Gregson, but it comes with the job." Grinning, she wiggled her brows.

Gemma shook her head and picked up her mug. She glanced at the screen again and almost choked on her tea. Sputtering her sip, she lowered the mug. On screen, in vivid color, were photos of the first few days of filming from *Starlight*, the upcoming summer blockbuster movie she'd auditioned for and lost out on. Too many times, she'd been told she "wasn't quite right for the role." And lately, the rejections cut deeper than they ever had before.

Jocelyn switched the channel back to the sports

network and lowered the volume. "I'm sorry. If I'd known they were going to show shots of the filming, I'd never have turned it on."

Tucking her hair behind her ears, Gemma inhaled a deep breath to quell the frustration burning in her blood. "When I arrived in LA, I told myself that if I hadn't made my big break by the time I turned thirty, I'd pack up and go home. I have one month left."

"You don't have to end your dream just because of an arbitrary deadline you invented."

"Not all dreams come true. And maybe it's time for me to face that mine might not either. I don't want to be a struggling actor anymore. LA is so expensive. Making ends meet is hard, even with the catering job, and now, I don't even have that. I don't know what to do." Something brushed against her leg, and then Bear's head bumped her knee. She reached down and petted his soft fur and accepted his comfort.

"I'm sorry." Jocelyn watched her for a moment, brows drawn together. Her fingers drummed against the wooden table and then, with a slowly-forming smile, she sat back in her seat. "For as long as you're here, you can come to work for me."

Gemma huffed out a laugh. An image of herself in a hardhat and work boots, carrying around a two-by-four, flashed through her mind. "I don't have any experience swinging a hammer."

"No, silly, not as part of the construction crew. We provide lunches to them when they're working on one of the Caring Home Repair houses. I've been handling the job for my aunt while she recovers from hip surgery. You can take over making the food. Since you have experience in catering, your stuff will taste a lot better than what I've been slapping together. It really would help me out a lot, and it will give you a paycheck."

Adam's jacket hung on the back of her chair. Gemma plucked at the down fabric. Lending her a coat was one thing, letting her work for his company was another. "I don't know. What do you think Adam will say?"

"He'll be fine with it. Don't worry about him." With a careless toss of her hand, Jocelyn stood and cleared the soup bowls from the table.

But she did worry. *There's a difference between surviving and being okay.* His words at the plunge echoed through her head. Something was wrong, she could feel it. On the television, the image of a baseball diamond filled the screen. "Now that your dad is doing so well, do you think Adam will head back to Sacramento?"

Jocelyn shook her head and then shrugged. "I asked a couple of times about spring training, but he's been very noncommittal about it. I don't know, maybe he's worried about my dad taking on too much again at work."

"Maybe." But she didn't think so. His pained expression, hardened stare, and sharp words all hinted at something more. Even though they weren't together, she couldn't turn off her old feelings like she hoped she could. Her need to care for him, to care about him, lingered like his aftershave on his jacket.

―――

The next day, after a morning spent in Jocelyn's kitchen, Gemma pulled her rental car up to the address her friend had scrawled across the back of an old receipt. A flurry of activity spread out before her. Two men fixed a broken porch, while several others replaced windows. A few glanced her way, then went back to their duties. She opened her door and turned to Bear in the passenger seat. "You wait here while I unload the food. Then we'll introduce you to the crew."

Jocelyn's SUV pulled up a minute later. She climbed out and pulled a small table from the back. "We'll set up right here. It's out of the crew's way."

Gemma carried the sandwiches to the table. A far cry from the fancy food she'd help create for events and parties, assorted rolls stuffed with turkey, chicken, and ham lined her trays. Then, she pulled out two kinds of pasta salad, a green salad, a carafe of coffee, and a cooler filled with sodas and bottled water.

"Whoa," Jocelyn's eyes rounded. "After seeing this spread, the guys are never going to want me making lunches again."

"Too much?" Scanning the workers, she spotted Adam at the window on the second floor, talking to another man. When his face creased into a smile, her heart beat a little faster. To see that smile again... If only it were aimed at her. "Adam was okay with me working for you guys?"

"I, ah, didn't get the chance to tell him yet." A blush stained Jocelyn's cheeks. She grabbed a can of soda from the cooler.

"Jocelyn." The wind carried away her sharp whisper. Gemma pushed her hands through her hair. Discomfort crawled through her stomach. No way did she want to be caught in the middle.

Beaming a smile at the workers, Jocelyn waved them

over to the table. "Adam will be fine. You working here won't be a problem for him."

Gemma returned her focus to the window and right into Adam's stare. From the tight expression darkening his features, he obviously had a big problem with it.

CHAPTER FOUR

Adam looked out the window he'd just finished installing. On the street below, Gemma stood with Jocelyn in front of the lunch table. Her long dark hair blew in the wind and settled over the shoulders of a bright blue peacoat he recognized as his sister's. Tight jeans showcased her trim legs. Her gaze met his, and a stab of desire flared to life. What was she doing at his job site?

An alert went off on his phone. He glanced at the text message on the screen. Dom Torres, the outfielder for the Los Angeles Riptide and the batter whose line-drive caused Adam's injury, had become a friend in the months since the incident.

Dom: Heard you received some invites for Spring Training. Looking forward to seeing you out on the mound again, buddy.

At thirty-two years old, this would likely be his last shot at playing in the major league. The nagging concern of not being able to shake his lack of control on the mound ate away at him, day after day. Rubbing the scar on his eyebrow, Adam replied with a "thanks," then tucked the phone in his pocket.

A flash of blue outside the window caught his attention. Gemma chatted with a few members of his crew as she handed out sandwiches.

The bright blue color was the same shade as the bikini she'd worn when they'd met at a polar plunge five years earlier. He'd immediately been interested. They'd set their belongings near each other and chatted while waiting for the plunge to begin. Their first date involved warming up with coffee after the plunge. They'd participated in another plunge the following winter, holding hands, wrapped in each other's arms. Warming up after that one included a steamy shower for two at his apartment.

Stop. He didn't need those thoughts seeping into his head.

He turned away from the window and sidestepped tools and crew members as he made his way through the rooms. Several members of the Hunter's Peak Trappers, the town's minor league baseball team and the same team that had given Adam his start, made up part of his crew. Minor league salaries fell far below their major league counterparts. He couldn't think of a single player or manager who didn't have a second job in the off-season. The fact that Hudson Contractors was able to employ them was a source of pride for him and his father.

Adam called out to Connor Muldoon, centerfielder for the Trappers and the hardest-working member of his crew. "Lunch break. Up for some batting practice after work today?"

"Sounds good." His friend took off his work gloves and followed him.

Adam owed Connor for trying to help him through his slump. Pitching sessions with him showed Adam hadn't lost his velocity. If he could overcome his mental block and stop throwing wild pitches, he might stand a shot at regaining his place on a team.

They stepped through the front door. The cold air stung exposed skin and chilled the sweat worked up over a full morning of manual labor. The tails of his thermal-lined flannel jacket kicked up in the wind. Gemma stood at the table, handing out sandwiches. The tip of her nose had turned pink. Dark hair spilled out from underneath a white knit hat. Silky strands danced around her face and tempted him with the memory of how they'd felt sliding through his fingers.

Connor's voice turned into a buzzing in his ear. He shook his head and forced his concentration back on his buddy. "Sorry. What?"

"I thought of a way to streamline the order system. Mind if I run it by your sister when I get back to the office?"

"Anything to speed up the paperwork would be great. Jocelyn's head is swimming with the amount we have now."

"Cool. I'll talk to her." He looked at the lunch table and grinned. "Lunch looks great today."

Adam's jaw clenched. Connor had better not be looking at Gemma. He turned to face his friend. Connor's eyes were stuck, gleaming, on the array of food covering the table. Relief flowed fast. He relaxed his muscles. And then his gaze locked on a pair of violet eyes fringed by thick lashes. Those eyes haunted him. He saw them every time he closed his own.

Beautiful didn't begin to describe her. Exotic, enchant-ing, with the mix of dark hair, pale skin, and an oval face carved to perfection. Her scent, a blend of flowers and something spicy, beckoned him closer. As if caught under a spell, he crossed to Gemma.

Deep barking came from the car behind her. She opened the car door, and a large dog bounded out and stood by her side. Gone was the small bundle of black and white fur they'd helped rescue four years earlier. The dog now likely outweighed Gemma. Adam slowed his steps.

He hung back as she let Bear sniff and familiarize himself with his surroundings. Amid the crew's exclama-tions of Bear's resemblance to a wolf or an actual bear, Adam stepped into the small crowd forming around the lunch table. Bear's ears perked up. He turned toward Adam, tugged on the leash, and nearly pulled Gemma off her feet. Something deep in his chest twinged when he locked eyes with the dog. A reminder of the love and dreams he had with Gemma when they'd rescued Bear from horrible living conditions, promising to take care of him. And each other.

The crowd fanned out, still peppering Gemma with questions. Adam crouched down and rubbed the dog's fur. "Hey, buddy. I missed you."

Bear whined and barked and jumped, resting his paws on Adam's shoulders. He hugged his dog and the feeling that this wasn't the way life was supposed to turn out flashed through him, hot and uncomfortable. Nudging the dog down, he rose and looked at Gemma. A shaky smile graced her lips. He could do this. Pushing the feelings aside to examine later, he offered one of his own. "Joce-lyn's making you work during your visit?"

His sister jumped to his side, the light of battle in her eyes. "I hired her. Gemma made lunch today. She's filling in until Aunt Gretchen comes back."

No. He didn't want her here, getting into his head. He wanted her back in LA, where he wouldn't have to think about her every single second. "Researching for a new role?"

The corners of her mouth turned down for a split-second. "Something like that."

Connor leaned over the table, drawing her attention with a question about Bear. She flashed him a smile, but it didn't reach her eyes. The dog stood patiently by her side, allowing Connor to pet him. No longer a hyper-active puppy. No longer the dog Adam remembered.

Jocelyn smacked his arm. "Help me get something out of the car."

He followed her to the street. The sounds from the crew's lunch break echoed through the quiet afternoon. "The hiring decisions are supposed to be made by both of us. Why is Gemma here?"

"She's upset. She doesn't know what to do with her life, and is wondering if it's time to throw in the towel on the whole acting thing."

"Seriously?" The declaration hit him like a bucket of ice water. Of all the possible reasons for her to be back in town, he hadn't expected that one.

From thirty feet away, he could see Gemma's stiff posture, and how her hands dug into Bear's leather leash. Shadows darkened her eyes. She kept pressing her lips together, a tell-tale sign that she was unsure of something.

"She's overwhelmed, and she's homesick. She couldn't even scrape together the money for the flight here. Things in LA aren't getting easier. She's out of a job and thinks she's too old to continue to pursue acting."

His gaze ranged over Gemma's delicate features. She'd chosen Los Angeles and a life that didn't include him, but after they'd ended their relationship, he'd still followed her career. He'd hoped the minor roles in low-budget movies would turn into something bigger for her. She was talented. Why couldn't Hollywood see what was obvious to him? "I had no idea things were so tough."

Jocelyn laid her hand on his shoulder. "You guys were really close once, maybe you can help her."

He dropped the guard back down over his heart. "That relationship's over."

"I'm simply saying she needs a friend. So, be nice to her." Concern creased his sister's face. Her hands rested on her hips. Her attempt at his father's my-way-or-the-highway stance usually brought a smile to his lips. But not today.

"I have to get back to work."

"You haven't eaten yet." Jocelyn grabbed his arm in the death-grip hold he'd taught her. "I hate seeing her so upset. Please, will you just talk to her?"

He detached her arm in a counter move. Jocelyn would keep pestering him until he finally gave in and agreed. He might as well get something out of it. "Fine. But you'll owe me something huge."

CHAPTER FIVE

Adam strode to the table. Gemma stood alone, with her arms wrapped around her middle, watching Connor toss a tennis ball to Bear. Her chin tucked close to her chest, her huddled posture, and the uncertainty in her expression begged for comfort or reassurance. He knew exactly how she felt, facing the impending end of a career, feeling old among the starry-eyed, fresh-faced newbies.

She met his gaze. The desire to wrap his arms around her, draw her into his strength, and hold her tight burned through his muscles. His hands curled into fists as he fought the sensation. He'd say his piece and then walk away.

"This is some spread." He picked up a sandwich. "Have you eaten?"

"I figured I'd make sure the crew had enough first before I dug in." She studied him with wary eyes. "I don't want to cause problems between you and Jocelyn. I'll leave if you want me to go."

Despite how their relationship ended, he couldn't toss her out knowing she didn't have a job. He'd figure out a way to deal with seeing her on a daily basis. Biting into the turkey on whole-wheat, he tasted Thanksgiving in a sandwich. "Are you kidding? This is the best thing I've eaten all year."

"We're only one month into the year." But her eyes lit up with his praise. The lines of tension on her face relaxed.

Ignoring the magnetic pull of her smile, he snagged a second sandwich and handed it to her. Too many members of his crew milled around them. "Come inside the house for a minute. I need to talk to you, and it's a little warmer in there."

"Oh no—your coat." She raised her hand to her forehead, then shook her head and muttered something about being too busy. "I forgot to bring it with me. The one you're wearing doesn't look as warm as the one you let me use."

"I'm hanging in there. Let's go." He cast a glance over his shoulder at Jocelyn. She gave him a thumbs-up sign, and he groaned. The last thing he needed was his baby sister trying to play matchmaker. Payback for this favor just tripled.

"What about Bear?" Gemma bit her lip and shifted her weight from one foot to the other. A gust of wind tossed strands of hair around her face.

"Jocelyn and Connor will keep an eye on him."

"All right. But only for a few minutes. I don't want them to think we stuck them with dog-sitting duty."

After grabbing a coffee and a bottle of water, he led Gemma into the house. The smell of sawdust filled the air.

Planks of wood, sawhorses, and power drills created an obstacle course through the first floor.

She spun in a slow circle. "Wow, you guys are doing a lot of work in here."

"Repairing something you know how to fix is easy." Houses were simple—he could repair almost anything. Pitching had been simple once, too.

They settled side by side on the bottom of the stairs. Their thighs brushed together, but neither he nor Gemma moved away. "It's been a while since we shared a meal."

"Yep." She opened the bottle and took a sip of water. A droplet hung on her lower lip until her tongue darted out and captured it.

Forcing his gaze away from her mouth required monumental effort. "How are things in LA?"

Spots of color appeared on her cheeks. Her gaze fell to her lap. "I'm guessing Jocelyn already told you."

He took another bite out of the sandwich. After he swallowed, he lifted his brow. "Things are tough out there. I get it."

Hands paused on the sandwich wrapper, she stared at him for a moment, her expression eloquent. "I'm not sure you do."

"Then tell me." His knee nudged her leg. "You used to be able to tell me anything."

"I'm not where I thought I'd be. At all. In anything." She ripped off a piece of the bread and raised her gaze to his. "Admitting failure is the hardest part. Especially to you."

Her words caught him in the center of his chest. A direct echo of his feelings.

When he reached the majors, he'd immersed himself in the game, driven by an all-consuming need for success. He'd worked hard for himself, but a large part of him was doing it for Gemma, too. He'd wanted to be able to offer her the world. Knowing that she was aware of his fall from grace rubbed more dirt into the wound.

Opening up to her, as hard as it was, might help her to feel better. "You want to talk about not being where you thought you'd be? Try going from being a pitcher known for his accuracy, known for hardly ever walking a batter, to being a rehabbing pitcher who couldn't pull his game together. I was walking too many guys, throwing too far outside of the strike zone, and not putting the ball over the plate. Hell, I deserved to be benched."

Her fingers rested on his forearm. The touch—warm, the contact—electrifying and comforting. "Why did your game change so much? The sports reports stated you didn't have any brain trauma from the fracture, and that the concussion symptoms went away. They said the doctors gave you a clean bill of health."

"My head's healed. Physically, anyway. That line drive happened so fast, I didn't have time to react. When you pitch, you're hunched over, vulnerable for a few seconds to a ball smacked right back to you." He rolled his shoulders to relax the stiffness. His skin heated. "I hesitate, and my muscles tense up. The idea that the injury could happen to me again, and that it could do permanent damage is on my mind all of the time."

A light of understanding dawned across her face. "You can't play that way."

"You have to go out there with a no-fear attitude."

Anything less would surely throw the final out in his baseball career.

"I've never known you to be afraid of anything."

Afraid.

He hated that word. He hated the weakness.

She sighed. "To put my situation in baseball terms, I feel like I've been standing at the plate for twenty pitches, and I keep fouling into the stands."

Somehow, they ended up shoulder to shoulder and hip to hip. Gemma's hand lightly squeezed his arm. Adam stared at the elegant, tapered fingers that had once provided comfort, security, and passion, and covered her hand with his. "No matter what type of pitch life throws at you, only you can know when it's time to hang up your cleats or retire your glove."

"Is it time for you?"

Shrugging, he pushed down the sick feeling that accompanied the thought of being forced to walk away from the game for good. "I don't want it to be."

"You'll get your pitches fixed. I know it." Confidence coated her words. Her hand turned under his, and she linked their fingers.

He gave in to the urge to stroke the dark silk of her hair. Rich, black strands slipped through his fingers, and he remembered how it looked fanned out across his pillow. Needing more, his fingertips skimmed her temple. "I never liked seeing you upset."

Her head tilted closer to his. "Me, neither, about you. I guess that's why we fit so well together."

Closer, closer. Parts of his body chanted for him to lean in and taste her lips, to see if the magic was still there.

Heavy footsteps thumped across the porch and were

followed by a loud knock on the front door. Biting back a swear, Adam lowered his hand from Gemma's face. As the door swung open, he stood, and keeping their hands linked, pulled her to her feet.

Connor entered the room. "Fred's here."

"What's Dad doing here?" Adam grabbed the rest of his sandwich and released his hold on Gemma. The interruption saved him. Kissing Gemma wouldn't solve any problems, it would only create more.

Before he could walk outside, his father walked in, with Jocelyn and Bear at his side. "I wanted to see how the project was coming along."

In the months since his heart attack, he had grown stronger every day. Adam did whatever he could to ensure his dad's stress level stayed low and that he abided by the cardiologist's orders for a reduced workload.

"Sure, let's take a look." Downing the contents of his coffee cup allowed time for his system to settle and his mind to shift from thoughts of Gemma to thoughts of project deadlines.

Jocelyn handed Bear's leash to Gemma and linked her arm around their dad's waist. "I'll help, Daddy. I don't want you overdoing anything."

"I'm not an invalid." His smile took the sting out of the words.

Gemma walked toward the door, but Bear veered to the right and closer to the stairs. A soft sigh slipped out when Bear pulled her off course. She tugged on the leash. "Come on, we're going outside now."

Telling himself he simply wanted to spend more time with the dog, Adam stopped her by slipping the leash out of her hand. "You should come, too. We'll show you what projects are left so you can provide the right fuel for tomorrow's lunches for the crew."

She rewarded him with a smile, and for a moment, it was as though the separation of the last four years hadn't happened at all.

CHAPTER SIX

Gemma sat next to Jocelyn, in the passenger seat of her friend's SUV, hands cupped around a travel mug of coffee, as they inched along in bumper-to-bumper traffic. Late afternoon sun dipped low, casting streams of pinks and purples across the sky. A song about reunited lovers played from the car's speakers, and further cemented Adam as the focus of her concentration.

The way their hands had linked together, the way they'd almost kissed, played through her mind on continual repeat. The pull of him, the draw, was so hard to resist, but was it worth the risk of getting burned?

He hadn't been at the job site when she'd arrived with lunch earlier in the day. Jocelyn had mentioned that the firm's other projects kept him busy elsewhere. The stab of disappointment lingered longer than she'd expected.

Jocelyn heaved a sigh and turned off the main road. "Thanks again for coming with me. My dad likes us to have an extra person with us when we interview prospective families."

"No problem. After all you've done for me, I'm happy I was able to do something for you. I liked watching how you picked the next family to benefit from the home repair fund."

"I'm sorry the trip back is taking so long. We should have been home over an hour ago."

"I just hope Bear's behaving himself and not causing trouble. Connor was sweet to keep an eye on him so I could go with you. I don't want him to regret it." She glanced at the clock. Bear didn't like being apart from her for long periods of time. The vet's diagnosis of separation anxiety solved the mystery of why her sweet pet turned into a destructive animal when she wasn't around.

"Please, those guys love having Bear at the job site." Jocelyn pulled into the Hudson Contractors office parking lot. The building's inside lights were off.

Gemma scanned the empty parking lot. "Connor said he'd meet us here. Do you think they got stuck at the site?"

Jocelyn pulled out her phone and dialed. Within seconds, Connor's voice came on the line. "Hello?"

"Hey." She put him on speaker. "Where are you and Bear?"

"I got called in to bartend tonight, so Adam said he'd take Bear home. He stopped by the site right after you left."

Gemma gripped her mug and turned to Jocelyn. "Where does he live?"

She pocketed her phone. "He bought the Old Miller cabin, up on Hidden Road."

"I have to get there. Bear's been with him for hours now. The last time we were apart for this long, he broke down my kitchen door and destroyed the pantry."

The engine revved as Jocelyn swung the car out of the parking lot. "We'll be at my place in five minutes. You can grab your car and head up. I'd go with you, but I have a date tonight."

After stopping at Jocelyn's to pick up her car and Adam's coat, Gemma drove through town. The winding road led her up a steep incline, through a thick thatch of towering pines until finally, the house came into view. Light streamed from a few windows on the lower level of the large, rustic log cabin.

She parked in the driveway and surveyed the place he called home. Remote, private, and surrounded by trees. Frosty winds whistled through the branches. She grabbed his coat from the back seat, and then rushed up the walk and knocked on the door. No response. She knocked again, harder. Still no response.

When the wind died down, faint strands of rock music pulsed in a steady beat. Following the sound, she stamped her numbing toes around to the back of the house. Light gleamed from a room constructed mostly of windows. Gemma peered inside.

A treadmill, an elliptical machine, free weights, and a rowing machine filled the space. Bear lay on the floor in the corner. He was safe and behaving himself. Nothing appeared ripped up or destroyed. Her anxiety eased.

In the room's center, Adam stood, shirtless, lifting weights. Blue sweatpants with the Storm's logo hung low on his hips. Sweat dripped down his chest. Sculpted muscles flexed with every repetition.

Her fingers itched to touch. Her body remembered, too well, how his strength used to surround her. Thinking about that wouldn't help now. She rapped on the window hard enough to shake the glass. The weights fell to the floor, and he whipped around. His glare faded with recognition and lightened into a smile. He jerked his thumb toward the front of the house. Pinpricks of nervous energy dotted her skin. She jogged to the front door.

When Adam opened the door, warmth and light flowed out. He tugged a sweatshirt over his torso. "Thanks for bringing that back."

She handed over his coat. "We were stuck in traffic. I'm so sorry you had to take Bear home with you."

Bear pushed past Adam's legs. She knelt to accept the dog's greeting, then stood, and grabbed hold of his collar. "Did he behave himself?"

"He's been great. I like having him around."

"Are you sure he didn't damage anything? Maybe you should double-check." Images of ruined shoes, chewed up couches, and ransacked rooms jumped into her mind. "He can get pretty destructive if I'm away from him for too long."

Adam beckoned her inside. "Come in. See for yourself."

He set his coat on a chair, and she slipped off her own. The rustic theme continued inside the house with wide-planked polished wooden floors and walls, vaulted ceilings with exposed wooden beams, and a large stone fireplace in the living room. "Nice place."

"I bought it two years ago. My escape from California." He shrugged and led her into the kitchen. Appliances gleamed from either obsessive cleaning or lack of use. Judging by Adam's behavior when they were together, Gemma voted for the latter.

"Drink?"

"Sure. Coffee, if you have it." So far, nothing appeared damaged. She mentally applauded her dog for his good behavior.

Bear stood in front of her, tilted his head, and let out two short barks. She glanced at Adam. "He needs to go out."

"Let me grab his leash first. The yard isn't fenced in." He ducked out of the room, then returned a few moments later and handed her the leash and her coat.

Murmuring a thanks for this thoughtfulness, she slid into the coat and secured the leash to Bear's collar. "All set."

Adam opened the door to the backyard. A rush of cold air blasted into the room. Bear pulled her to the middle of the yard, then stopped and nosed his way around the wide open space.

Gemma wrapped her arms around her middle and shifted her weight from one foot to the other in a useless attempt to ward off the chill. The cold didn't seem to bother Adam as much. He stood, legs splayed, arms crossed, as he watched Bear.

After a few minutes, she tugged the leash. "Let's go, boy."

Bear trotted to her, then danced away. They went through the charade twice more before she threw up her arms and turned to Adam. "I'm sorry. When he gets like this, I usually leave him out for a bit. It's easier than trying to pull him away. You can go in if you want."

He pointed to the stake in the ground on the side of the yard. "The previous owners left this. We can attach the leash to it so Bear can run around, and we can stay warm."

She secured the dog and followed Adam inside the

house. He gave her the tour of the rooms Bear had visited. In his den, several baseball trophies lined one wall. She walked closer to examine them. Behind one, a photo of herself stuck out, tucked between the trophy and a baseball.

"What's this?" She pulled out the picture. It was of her and Adam. They stood on the pitcher's mound at the Trappers' field, their arms wrapped around each other. The stadium was empty, but the lights were still on. The scoreboard behind them spelled out: *Congratulations Adam. Good luck in the show.*

The memory of that night came back to her. During the game, word had come down that he'd been called up to the majors to pitch for the Storm. One of his teammates mentioned the news to the scoreboard guy, and as soon as the game ended, the sign had lit up the field.

She raised her gaze to his face. "I remember that night."

"Me, too. Celebrating with you was the best part." He stood so close to her, she could feel the warmth from his skin. When his hand closed over her shoulder, a reminder of how much she missed his touch, she nearly leaned into him.

"That was a long time ago." He'd left for Sacramento the following day, and in the weeks that followed, never asked her to join him. If he'd loved her, he would have. She tucked the photo back in its place and glanced out the window. Daylight had faded, and clouds rolled in. "I have to go."

He nodded and stepped back. She kept glancing at him as they walked into the kitchen. How much had changed over the years and how much stayed the same?

The back door opened with a faint squeak. Braced for the cold, she stepped into the yard. Bear wasn't there. His leash lay on the ground by the stake, the metal clasp attachment for the collar broken. A chill spread over her skin to the deepest parts of her bones. "Bear?"

No jingling collar, no excited bark. No sign of her dog. Her stomach dropped and then iced with fear. Cupping her hands around her mouth, she yelled, "Bear?"

Adam came up behind her.

She turned around. "He never wanders off."

"There are a million new smells and things for him to investigate here. Maybe he saw a fox."

A wolf's howl, sounding all too close, sent shivers down her spine. "He's out there all alone. What if he gets attacked? I have to find him."

She started for the woods.

"Wait." Adam's hand closed around her forearm. "We need coats and flashlights."

Her about-face brought her into his chest. She inhaled his familiar scent and comfort battened down the worry rumbling in her head. "You're coming with me?"

He stared at her, brow cocked as though she'd just asked the most basic question in the world. "Coats, hats, and gloves. Now."

She rushed inside and tugged on her coat. Her fingers fumbled with the buttons. "He's not used to this weather."

"He has a thick fur coat. He's probably loving the snow." Adam handed her a flashlight and then pulled a red knit cap over her hair.

"I know, I know, but he's not used to these surroundings. He's been with me every day for the last four years. I don't want anything to happen to him." Impatient, she waited while he zipped up his jacket and tugged on gloves. "Let's go."

He reached into a closet and thrust a pair of gloves three sizes too big into her hands. "Wearing them is a better option than getting frostbite."

Within seconds, they returned to the yard. Adam beamed his flashlight over the snow-covered lawn. Paw prints ran in circles around the stake, then a single set headed into a cluster of pines. "We'll find him. There's a hiking trail over here. Looks like he headed that way."

They followed the prints. Snow crunched under her feet. The longer they walked on the trail, the thicker the woods became. Stinging, strong winds blew in their faces, stealing breath, carrying away their calls, slowing their progress. Thick snowflakes began to fall.

Wolves howled in the distance. Could Bear defend himself if he crossed paths with one? Could they? Gemma aimed her flashlight at the trees, then looked over her shoulder. The scene seemed too silent, too still, like something hidden in the shadows waited to pounce. The hair on the back of her neck lifted. She shifted closer to Adam's side. "They hunt in packs, don't they?"

He stopped walking and caught her hand in his. "I won't let anything happen to you, or Bear. I promise." The determination in his voice and the intensity of his gaze inspired her to believe him. He wrapped his arm around her shoulders. "We'll find him."

The path widened and curved around a section of boulders taller than Adam. Gemma leaned into his steady support and ducked her head against the wind.

"Bear." Adam's voice snapped in a low, harsh tone. His hand curled around her arm and halted her progress.

"Where is he?" She raised her head.

Her elation turned to fear.

Thirty feet in front of them, a black bear stood on its haunches.

Her mind screamed that this was winter, and bears should be hibernating. At once, information on how to survive an encounter flooded through her brain. Growing up in the Catskills, the likelihood of encountering a bear was a real concern. It had never happened to her, and the sight of the animal so close to them paused her heartbeat. Her limbs locked and her body refused to obey her mind's commands.

The bear dropped down on all fours and swatted the ground with its front paw.

Adam shifted in front of her and widened his shoulders. "Don't make eye contact. Tilt your head down."

Gemma's muscles tensed, and she fought the urge to run. Running wasn't smart. "Adam."

His head didn't turn to look at her. "Turn sideways at an angle. Back up, slow. No sudden movements. No running." His firm command seemed to be addressed to both her and the animal.

Keeping one hand on the back of Adam's coat, she glanced over her shoulder and took a step back. Her dog's prints veered off the trail. Hopefully, he was safe. A branch cracked beneath her feet. Her heart pounded so hard, she thought it might come out of her chest.

Two more slow steps back.

Adam's build blocked out her view of the bear, but she could hear it swatting the ground and snorting. "Keep going, nice and slow."

More leaves rustled and something crashed through the

forest, much closer to them. Fear of a second bear, or a wolf, filled her. She gripped the flashlight and held it over her head, prepared to swing.

With a growl, a familiar black and white body burst out of the trees. Bear stood ten feet in front of her and Adam, growling and barking at the bear. The bear swatted the ground again.

Gemma pushed forward a few steps. "I have to get him. Bear, stop!"

"No." Adam's hands clamped onto her arms and jerked her into his chest. "Stay with me."

The Akita continued to bark and howl and growl.

Adam's voice rumbled in her ear, "Keep backing up with me."

Her hand lifted to his arms. She gripped tight and allowed his movements to guide her steps. The standoff between her pet and the wild animal continued in snarls and growls. Finally, the bear retreated into the woods.

Adam whistled for the dog. Bear backed up toward them, keeping his face turned toward the direction the bear had gone. Adam's fingers tightened a fraction more on her arms. "Let's move. Keep it slow."

With shaking fingers, Gemma grabbed hold of Bear's collar. Her limbs felt like jelly. She concentrated on staying on the path, ears primed for sounds of anything other than the crunch of snow under their feet. The snowflakes fell thicker and faster, swirling and making it hard to see.

When they passed the curve in the path, Adam turned and faced her. Tension lined his face. His gloved hand grasped hers tight. "We should be fine now."

Her breaths still came too quick. "How did that happen? It's winter. Bears should be hibernating."

"Females give birth in January. I've heard stories of sows walking outside their dens when having labor pains. They're more likely to attack because they're agitated. We were lucky."

Lucky.

She squeezed his hand and held on as they continued walking. Focusing on taking deep breaths, she kept looking over her shoulder, waiting for the bear to reappear. Finally, Adam's home came into view. Relief seeped into her system.

They reached the back door. Bear nudged against her side and cocked his head. She dropped to her knees and wrapped her arms around him, burying her face in his fur. "Such a brave boy. But don't ever run away again."

Then she stood and turned to Adam. Like Bear, he'd put himself in front of her. Emotions tripped over each other. Words weren't enough to express her thanks. She wrapped her arms around him and held on tight.

CHAPTER SEVEN

Adam wrapped his arms around Gemma and willed his system to settle. The encounter with the bear could have met a much more gruesome end. He couldn't stop the images bombarding his mind. By some manner of luck, they'd stayed safe. Lucky didn't begin to cover the way he felt. The need to hold onto Gemma was as vital as the need to breathe. He couldn't let her go.

Some twist of fate brought her back into his life.

She still mattered. More than he'd thought.

He still cared. More than he'd imagined.

He wanted a second chance.

In the four years they'd been apart, he'd felt like a part of him was missing. An emptiness that nothing could chase away. Gemma was the missing piece. Holding her, being with her, clicked everything back into perfect balance. Now, he just had to convince her to take a chance on him.

Pressing a kiss to the top of her head, he unlocked the door.

She stopped at the doorframe and grabbed hold of Bear's collar. "We've caused you enough trouble for one night. We should go."

Bear pulled her forward, over the threshold and into the house.

"Come on, boy, we have to get home." She planted her feet and tugged, but Bear turned into an immovable statue.

Adam shook his head. "You should stay a while. After that encounter, I need a drink." Or five. "I'm guessing you do, too."

"I could use a drink. And I need to return your hat and gloves." She released her hold on Bear's collar. He shook himself, turned in three circles, and then took off down the hall. The sound of paws skittering as they hit hardwood floors followed his zig-zagging path to the kitchen.

Laughing over the dog's antics, she turned back to him, eyes bright, cheeks rosy, and lips curved in a perfect smile.

Finding breathing difficult, Adam reached out. "I'll help."

With gentle fingers, he pulled the hat off her head, then he removed the gloves one at a time.

Gemma's quick intake of breath broke the silence. He locked eyes with her, and the intensity of her gaze sent a rush of heat through his body.

Making an effort to relax his stiffening muscles, he slowly lowered the zipper, and then pushed the coat off her shoulders.

The fit of her blue sweater hinted at the curves hidden underneath. Understated and sexy.

His fingers brushed the underside of her chin. Her sigh and her soft skin encouraged him to continue.

"You looked cute in my gear." He trailed his fingers

down the side of her neck and dipped to trace the collar of her shirt.

Gemma laid her hands on his chest, her expression serious, and her voice soft and clear. "You put yourself in front of me out there, between the bear and me."

He'd moved on instinct. Protecting her was all that mattered. "I told you I'd keep you safe."

"Thank you." She lifted onto her toes and rubbed her cheek against his. "But just so you know, if anything had happened, I would have fought to protect you, too."

When she pulled back, her fingers curled into the front of his shirt. Her gaze searched his, then focused on his mouth, then raised to meet his again. Time apart hadn't weakened their connection. He couldn't stop the surge of his heartbeat. He tilted his head, leaning down, drawn to her. The delicate shiver that shook through her body snapped his focus to her comfort. "Let's get warmed up."

Wrapping his arm around her, he walked with her into the kitchen and started a fresh pot of coffee. While it brewed, Gemma told him stories of Bear's exploits over the years—the separation anxiety, the encounters with mail carriers, and the dog's insistence on being a lapdog regardless of his size.

A few minutes later, they settled in the den with cups of coffee laced with a shot of bourbon. Bear lay on the floor by their feet. As she drank her coffee, Gemma's eyes softened and the smile gracing her lips widened. Little by little, they shifted closer together, and the room's temperature ticked up a few degrees. The need to kiss her overwhelmed him. He set their cups on a side table. When he sat back, Gemma snuggled against him.

In the quiet room, the only sounds were the ticking of

the clock and their breathing. Violet eyes steady on his, Gemma laid her hand on his chest. His eyes briefly closed at the contact. No one compared to her.

He cupped her cheek with his hand and brushed his thumb across her lips. They parted under his touch. He fought against the need to rush. She was back in his arms, and he wanted to savor the moment. Adam moved in and gently pressed a kiss to her right cheek. Then, he placed a kiss on her left cheek.

He pulled back, a breath away, his pulse pounding. Her eyes locked on his, and she smiled. They watched each other as they slowly moved together and lips pressed against lips.

Testing.

Teasing.

Tasting.

Her scent, her taste, her feel, were all the same as before. The powerful punch of sensations overwhelmed him. Drawing back, he traced his finger down her cheek.

Whispering his name, she tilted her face toward his, her eyes filled with emotion. Adam slanted his lips over hers and shifted to a more comfortable position. His fingers on her neck urged her closer.

Gemma slid her hands around his back and held him tight. The soft curves of her chest and hips pressed against him.

He groaned. With one hand tangled in her hair and the other reaching under her shirt to caress the soft skin of her back, he opened himself to feelings and sensations he'd tried to bury.

She was as intoxicating as ever.

Bear leaped from the rug, and in one graceful move,

settled his one-hundred-twenty-pound bulk across their laps. Grunting under the weight, Adam pushed, trying to shift the dog's body off of Gemma.

Her laughter filled the room. "Sorry. He doesn't realize he's too big to be a lapdog. Bear, down."

Bear whined, but resumed his spot on the floor, this time, lying directly on their feet.

"This guy deserves a medal for bravery." Adam patted the soft fur.

"So do you." Gemma directed his lips back to hers, and he didn't care if ten more dogs piled on top of them. Kissing Gemma after such a long delay was better than any medal.

Better than anything else in the world.

CHAPTER EIGHT

Two days after the standoff with the bear, Gemma had a hard time letting her own Bear out of her sight. His protective guard stayed elevated, too. He followed her from room to room and stuck close to her side at the job site. Only Adam was able to coax him away. Games of catch followed each lunch hour, with Adam hurling baseballs into a field and Bear running to fetch them. Adam's love for the sport was obvious. She wished she knew of a way to help him with his game.

Standing in the warmth of the Hudson Contractors office, she organized a closet bursting with office supplies. Adam had taken Bear outside for a walk. Stretching her muscles, she crossed to his desk and looked at the calendar. Two weeks until spring training. He'd told her the East Coast teams held spring training in Florida, while the West Coast teams held theirs in Arizona.

What would happen when he left? If he left? She wasn't any closer to her decision on Hollywood. The realization that she hadn't given acting much thought in days hit her, and with weakened legs, she sank into Adam's desk chair.

What did she want?

The answer was immediate.

Him.

It had always been him. She'd screwed up once. She didn't want to mess things up again. A second chance didn't come around for everyone. But what if he didn't feel the same way?

A few kisses didn't mean he wanted her the way she wanted him. Even if they were pulse-scrambling, thought-scattering, blood-pumping kisses.

A few evenings together didn't mean he wanted her back in his life. Even if they were filled with flirting and laughter and a sense of rightness.

A few days filled with playful texts and quick calls didn't mean she was on his mind as often as he was on hers. Or did it?

He wasn't immune. Not with the way his body had heated and wrapped around hers, or the way his eyes crinkled when he smiled at her, or the way his voice shifted when he said her name.

She spun the chair in a slow circle.

Being cautious would be wise. Plunging headlong into something wouldn't be smart, no matter how *right* it felt. She wasn't the same girl who'd left Hunter's Peak four years earlier. Adam had changed, too.

Thinking about her future, making plans for her next step needed to be the focus of her attention. She loved acting too much to completely step away from it, but the thought of toiling away in LA for months or years was as appealing as another encounter with the bear.

Collar jangling, Bear trotted into the room and padded over to greet her. Like magic, her stress evaporated.

Adam entered a few seconds later, carrying a large stack of papers. "Thanks for organizing the closet."

"No problem. Need some help?"

"Can you grab a few rubber bands? They're in the top drawer on your right."

She pulled it open. Underneath a tangled pile of rubber bands and paper clips, the words *official* and *retirement* and *baseball* jumped out from a piece of paper. A heavy feeling settled over her stomach. Her fingers tingled as she held it out to him. "What's this?"

He set the papers on another desk, his expression unreadable. "I thought about retiring."

"But you love the game. I know you do. I've watched you pitch. And you're good." Desperate to make him see, she rattled off his statistics as a member of both the Trappers and the Storm. Though she'd never admitted it to anyone, she'd watched nearly every game of his major league career from the comfort of her apartment or the local sports bar. "You can't give up yet."

He rubbed his hands over his face. "There's more to it than my loving the game."

She scanned the document. When she reached the bottom, the tension clutching her muscles eased. "It says here that you have to mail this to the league."

"That's the way it works."

She ignored the sarcasm in his comment and pushed to her feet. "Look at the date on the paper. If you really wanted to retire, you'd have sent it in three months ago. Since you didn't, that tells me you still want to give playing a shot. And you should."

At his side, his hand curled into a fist. "Of course, I want to play. Do you have any idea how frustrating it is to want something so much but it's just beyond your reach?"

"Of course, I do. Every time I watched you pitch for the Storm, I felt that way." The words slipped out so fast, she couldn't stop them.

His jaw slackened. "What?"

The music she recognized as his cell phone's ringtone played from his pocket, but he didn't move to answer it. Body tense, he watched her with that steady, serious gaze she recognized from his playing days. After a long moment, his voice ground out, "How long did you feel that way?"

Would he think her weak? Pathetic? She had to be honest, no matter how vulnerable it left her. "Since the first game you pitched."

"Damn it." He pushed his hand through his hair and walked to the window. His features tightened into a brooding scowl. Muttering another swear word, he shook his head. "I've kicked myself for four years, blaming myself for being so focused on the game that I lost you."

Gemma's heartbeat ticked into overdrive. She couldn't believe what she was hearing. He blamed himself for losing *her*? She inhaled a deep breath that did nothing to soothe the nerves needling her stomach. "I hated being stuck here while you lived your dream. A dream that apparently didn't include me." The admission nearly choked her.

He stared at her while a vein in his neck pulsed. "I didn't know if the Storm would keep me or send me back down after a couple of games. I was a career minor-leaguer. I didn't have anything to offer you."

"Your heart would have been enough."

"Gemma." His eyes flared with heat. He reached for her, but she backed away, emotions ripped open, raw and exposed.

"Never mind. It's fine."

He stalked toward her until her back pressed against the filing cabinet. "Damn it, do you think you're the only one who wanted? Why do you think I concentrated so hard on playing ball? I wanted to be a success, for you, but by then it was too late. You were in LA and had a whole new life."

"I love acting, but rushing off to LA was a desperate move. I only headed there because you didn't ask me to go with you." Her cell phone's ringtone played from her purse. She glanced at it, then back into Adam's thunderous expression.

"You were photographed with other guys often enough. Ticked me off."

Her stomach knotted. "I thought you'd moved on, so I tried to do the same. Only I couldn't. No matter how many times I told myself to forget you, I couldn't."

The phone on his desk rang. Growling, he snatched it up. "Hudson Contracting."

Harsh passion drained, leaving an emotionless mask. Adam's hand tightened around the receiver. "I'll be right there."

"What's happened?" She crossed to his side in the span of a heartbeat. The urge to soothe whatever stressed him pulsed steady and strong. Stronger than any of the hurt she'd been feeling.

Dropping the phone on its cradle, he met her gaze. "My dad collapsed. They took him to the hospital."

CHAPTER NINE

Adam strode down the hospital hallway with Gemma at his side, her hand clasped in his. The stale scent of coffee and antiseptic lingered in the air. He hated the thought of his father—the man he'd idolized growing up, the man who'd taught him everything he knew about baseball—being sidelined by a weakening heart. He clenched his jaw against the flash of helplessness. This was one more thing he couldn't fix.

Speculating on what could be wrong wouldn't help anything. He needed to keep calm so he could develop a game plan for later. No matter what happened with base-ball, his family would come first. He'd make sure he provided whatever his dad needed.

Jocelyn met them in the hall. "Dad seems to be okay. The doctors are running tests."

Her voice was calm and even, but her hands twisted together, and her features pinched in worry. Grasping Gemma's hand tighter, Adam steeled himself for the worst and entered the room.

His father lay propped up in the bed, watching the TV. His coloring looked paler than normal. He gestured with the remote control. "My ticker better not be acting up again. I have a business to run."

"We'll take care of things for you, Dad, don't worry. How are you feeling?"

"The hospital doesn't carry a sports package. I'll miss the Maine and Ohio game tonight." In other words, he felt fine.

Adam's muscles relaxed. The breath he'd held released. "I'll bring you the game highlights tomorrow."

"I'd better be home by then."

One of the nurses came in, pushing a cart. Her yellow scrubs and warm smile brightened the sterile, white room. "I'm sorry, but I'll have to ask you all to wait in the hall for a minute."

Jocelyn glanced from Gemma to Adam. "I'm going on a coffee run. We'll be here a while."

Adam walked with Gemma to the empty waiting room at the end of the hall. When her fingers shifted against his, he realized he hadn't let go of her hand since they'd entered the hospital. She probably needed a break. With a monumental effort, he released his hold. And instantly felt the loss.

He needed her. Her touch. Her presence. Her support.

"I hate seeing him like this." Restlessness carried him to the window. The gray, overcast sky fit his mood perfectly.

"I know. I do, too." Gemma's soft voice matched the light touch she placed on his arm. "He'll be fine. He's a tough guy, like you."

"You're pretty tough yourself." She'd always been

strong for him, and he'd drawn from that to be everything she'd needed.

"No, I'm not." She wrapped her arms around her middle and walked to the center of the room. "This room reminds me too much of the one when you were in the hospital. The colors are the same."

His brows knitted together. The team had released a few photos of him smiling and holding a get-well card signed by the fans. But he'd been in his private room at the hospital, not the waiting room.

Her chest rose and fell with a deep breath. She turned and paced a few steps, then turned back to face him. "You don't know what it was like, watching them cart you off the field on a stretcher. Or seeing you lying in that hospital bed, with all of those machines beeping."

"You came to see me?" Breath caught in his lungs. As if on cue, his scar itched. "That's almost a six-hour drive from LA to Sacramento."

"I had to see you. I waited for the post-game report, but the team didn't know the extent of your injuries. People were speculating about brain damage. I was so worried. I drove up as soon as your coach ended his press conference. I sat with you for a while, until the nurse came in to do something and asked me to leave."

She sank into a chair. His heart beat uncomfortably. He crouched in front of her and laced his fingers with hers. "I swore I smelled your perfume in that hospital room. I thought I was hallucinating. Damn it. Why didn't you stay until I woke up?"

"When I came back, a woman was sitting on the bed, holding your hand, telling you everything would be okay." Her tone hesitant, she shifted her gaze to the floor.

"The only women who came to see me were my sister and a few of my teammates' wives. What did she look like?"

One delicate shoulder lifted in a half-shrug. "Tall and thin, with short blonde hair. She said she'd take care of you, and she wasn't wearing a wedding ring, so I thought—"

He held up his hand to cut her off. "That's Pattie. She's the catcher's wife. They lived next door to me. They helped me out a lot during my recovery."

"Oh." She pressed her lips together and her chin dipped down to her chest. Her hair fell forward, covering her face.

Heat radiated through his chest. She cared. His thumb stroked her knuckles. "You know, that confusion could have been solved by asking a simple question."

Her gaze shot to his. Pink flushed into her cheeks. "What was I supposed to do, waltz in there and demand that she explain who she was and her claim to you? We weren't dating. We hadn't even spoken since we'd broken up. I didn't have any right to interfere in your life. It was clear to me that you'd really moved on."

Before he could say anything, she pushed to her feet and walked a few steps away. Turning to face him, she dragged her hands through her hair. "All I could think was what a fool I'd been to drive up there to see you."

He shook his head and closed the distance between them. "Not a fool. If the situation were reversed, I'd have moved mountains to get to your side."

Eyes widened, she blinked. "Even after all the time we'd spent apart?"

They'd wasted four years because of pride. The thought irked him so much he wanted to push her away and at the same time, pull her close. "Even though we weren't together, I still kept tabs on you."

"Why?" She whispered, as though the question was too important, and the answer too scary, to speak out loud.

His hand captured hers. Standing in the middle of waiting room, he gave her the only thing he could—the truth. "You've always been the one."

CHAPTER TEN

The one? Gemma stared at him, her limbs frozen, her heart fluttering wildly. Hope and frustration and longing burned bright, each fighting for dominance. She swallowed against the thickness in her throat. "Adam."

His gaze locked on hers. Intensity poured off him in waves. "Ending things was a mistake."

Emotions tangled together. Elation swamped her. Then fear niggled in. They weren't the same people they were back then. Who knew how much had changed? What if they tried to get back together and failed? Or, one cared more than the other? Plus, too much remained uncertain about both of their futures.

"I've missed you." Adam's chest rose and fell in steady beats. Loose fists curled at his sides. Standing there, he looked so capable, so solid, so *right*.

Her arms ached to wrap around him. Even knowing how badly a broken heart had hurt, she couldn't lie. "I've missed you, too."

Relief flitted across his features. His hands clasped her shoulders. She strained to reach his mouth with hers.

The sound of footsteps interrupted them. Gemma turned toward the door. Jocelyn entered the room, holding a cardboard tray with three cups of coffee. She tilted her head to the side. "Am I interrupting anything?"

"What do you think?" Adam relaxed his hold and shifted Gemma to his side. He wrapped his arm around her waist.

She rested her hand against his chest and met Jocelyn's owlish gaze. Heat burned into her cheeks and cooled the happiness flooding her body. Their surroundings came back into focus. "We were just…"

Jocelyn nodded toward the hall. Her expression suggested she'd pump for details later. "The nurse said we can see Dad again."

Adam took a step toward the door but kept his arm snaked around Gemma, as though he had to maintain contact. "We're coming."

She leaned into his solid warmth as they walked down the hall. When they entered the room, Fred was talking to a doctor standing by his bedside. He waved them over and then pointed, "My daughter, Jocelyn, my son, Adam, and Gemma. She's a family friend."

After shaking hands with Jocelyn and Gemma, the doctor extended his hand to Adam. "I'm originally from Sacramento, so I'm a huge Storm fan. Are you ready for Spring Training?"

Beside her, Adam tensed. He didn't want to talk about it. Gemma curled her fingers around his waist and squeezed. She smiled at the doctor. "I'm sure the teams can't wait to get back to baseball. The weather in Florida and Arizona would be a nice change from the cold and snow up here."

"You've got that right. I spent the first two weeks of January surfing in Hawaii. Hated coming back to the cold weather." He rambled on about waves and hang times. After making a notation in the chart, he glanced at Fred. "I'll be back to see you in the morning."

Her diversion had worked. Adam's stance relaxed when the doctor left the room. He grabbed a coffee from the tray and slid his other hand from her waist to her neck and stroked her skin. Concentrating on the conversation between Jocelyn, Fred and Adam took superhuman effort.

Being his support felt good. If only she could figure out how to help him with his game.

After a night spent tossing and turning and thinking about Adam, Gemma rose early, fed Bear and took him for a walk. The cold air bit through her coat, but she didn't rush. If she kept walking, she might figure out a way to help him fix his game. He was running out of time.

An hour later, clutching a newspaper, she knocked on the doorframe of his father's hospital room. "How are you feeling?"

Fred waved for her to come inside. "Much better now. One of my medications needed to be adjusted, that's all. The doc said they'll discharge me this morning."

The sun streaming in through the window seemed to brighten. The wave of relief washed away her worry. "Thank goodness."

He nodded. "Adam will be back soon. He went home to grab a change of clothes for me."

Thinking about Adam, thinking about his admission, she sank into the bedside chair and handed his father the newspaper. "I brought the Sports section so you can read about the Maine and Ohio game."

"You're a good kid." Instead of opening the paper to the scoring recaps, he turned to the baseball section. "Spring training begins soon."

A winter hat with the Storm's logo perched on the top of the chair. She brushed her hand over the material. "I wonder what Adam will do."

"I taught him how to pitch, you know." Fred's chin lifted, and his eyes gleamed. "Everyone said he had a major league arm. He threw the ball hard but threw wild pitches in the beginning."

Like now. She leaned forward in her seat, her hands clasped together. "How did you correct it?"

"I set up a tire in the old barn behind the house. Told him to throw it through the circle in the middle. That's how he learned."

"Do you think it would work again?"

He rubbed his hand over his eyes and shrugged. "I brought it up to him when he came home from Reno but he didn't want to talk about pitching then. The problem was too new, too raw. Plus, he was focusing all his energy on running my company while I recovered. My kids really took care of me."

"Of course, they did." She patted his hand. "I know how important you are to them. Getting you healthy was all that mattered."

She eyed the door and rose. Adam could return any

minute, and she needed time to put her plan in place. "Do you know where I can get a tire and some rope?"

His father frowned. "It may not help him. His problem is mental not mechanics."

"But it's worth a shot."

Gathering the materials took less time than she'd anticipated. After picking up Bear from Jocelyn's house, she headed to Adam's home. Talking to the dog while she worked helped calm her nerves. An hour later, she heard a car pull into the driveway. Stepping back from her handiwork, she hurried into the front yard.

"Hey." Grinning, Adam climbed out of the car. He wrapped his arms around her. Bear barked and nudged their legs. Adam dropped his hand to the dog's head and rubbed. "This is a nice surprise."

"I have a better one. Come with me." She tugged his hand and moved a few steps toward the side of the house.

"What's going on?"

"You'll see." Her stomach clenched around a baseball-sized ball of nerves. Hopefully, he wouldn't be angry she had interfered. Before they reached the backyard, she paused and faced him. "In your career, you've had about twenty-five starts per year, and about one hundred pitches per game. You've played over ten years. So that's roughly twenty-five-thousand pitches."

He nodded. "That's about right."

"Now think about all the other pitchers in the league, all of the games they've pitched, all of the pitches they've thrown. How many times have they been hit by a pitch? You have a greater chance of being eaten by a shark, or being struck by lightning, than you do of getting hit by a come-backer like that again."

His brows raised. "Someone's been doing some statistics research."

"Just keep that in mind." She pulled him into the backyard. Bear raced ahead of them. On the largest tree, the tire she'd hung swayed from a bright red rope. "You learned to throw accurately this way before, so maybe it will work again."

He stared at the tire but didn't say a word.

She squeezed his hand and then let go. "When you're out there on the mound, you can picture the tire, not the catcher's mitt. Maybe that will help you."

Still, he didn't say anything. A muscle jumped in his jaw. He walked closer to the tree.

Staying rooted to her spot, she motioned for the dog to come to her side. "You aren't angry, are you?"

"You really want to help me." The quiet wonder in his voice pulled at something deep inside her.

"Of course, I do. I..." *Still love you. Never stopped loving you.* But she couldn't say it. Not yet. They'd never spoken those words to each other. He might not believe it, or worse, he might not say it back.

"You what?" He turned and faced her. His brows lifted, and the intensity of his gaze kept her pinned to her spot.

"I believe in you." That much was true. She forced her lips to curve. "Now let's go throw some baseballs."

Adam walked toward her, his long legs striding over the snow. His gloved hands covered her shoulders. His head swooped down and warm lips pressed against hers. A bolt of heat shot up her spine. Gemma slid her hands up his chest and over his shoulders. He trailed kisses over her cheek. "Thank you."

The words teased the strands of hair against the nape of

her neck. She shivered and snuggled in closer and returned her lips to his. Warm and soft, they teased hers apart and then his tongue slipped inside to tangle with hers. Arms as strong as steel beams banded around her back. Through his open coat, the hard plane of his chest and torso pressed against her body.

Her limbs weakened with wanting. She'd missed this. She'd missed him. She couldn't get close enough.

With a bark, Bear jumped between them, knocking her thigh with his head. Then he repeated the motion. Adam's chuckle was muffled against her mouth but she felt his lips lift in a smile. He reached one hand down to ruffled Bear's fur.

Breathing hard, she pulled away from Adam. "That was one heck of a warm up."

"I'm just getting started." His finger traced over her lip. A shudder tore through her body. "Wait here."

She adjusted her coat and rubbed Bear's back while she waited.

Adam returned a minute later holding a baseball and two baseball gloves. "Up for a little catch?"

She accepted the glove and slipped the soft leather over her hand. "I haven't done this in years."

"It'll come back to you." He jogged a short distance away, then lobbed the ball in her direction.

She raised her glove. Bear barked and tore across the yard. Knocking into her, he leaped and captured the ball in his teeth. Her foot slipped on a divot in the snow. She stumbled to the side but couldn't capture her balance. Cold, hard snow slammed into her elbow and hip.

"Whoa. Are you okay?" Adam's hands circled around hers. He helped her to her feet and brushed the snow off her jeans. His fingers lingered on her hip. "Does anything hurt?"

She rubbed her elbow. "I'm fine. He doesn't know his own strength."

Bear danced around them, tail wagging for more. He dropped the ball at their feet. Adam knelt beside him. "You need to be more careful with our girl, buddy."

Our girl? Her pulse quickened. He sent her a smile, then threw the ball across the yard. The dog took off after it.

Adam stood and cupped his hand around her jaw. "Sure you're okay?"

"Absolutely." She reached up and laid her hand over his. He looked at her with such care. Her insides turned to jelly.

His lips descended and teased against hers. The warmth of his body chased away the cold air. Too soon, he stepped back and pulled another baseball from his jacket pocket. "Let's try this again."

His mechanics, the wind-up, and the movement of his body were flawless. The ball flew out of his hand and arced in a straight path to her glove. The leather didn't lessen the sting of the ball slamming into her palm. She closed her other hand over the glove, capturing the ball. Smiling, she fired a shot back at him.

"Nice." He nipped the ball out of the air and then hurled a fastball at the tire. It sailed through the hole and landed at the edge of the yard.

"You did it." Squealing her cheer, she ran to him and threw her arms around his waist.

He smiled, and his hands grasped her waist. The pleasure lighting his features nearly took her breath away. "One ball through the tire doesn't mean anything."

"But it's a start."

Bear retrieved the ball and trotted to Adam. His tail wagged back and forth. Adam threw another perfect pitch through the tire. Again, Bear retrieved.

Adam continued to put ball after ball through the hole. Gemma stood close to his side, smiling so hard her cheeks hurt. With every pitch, her excitement grew. He looked like his old self—confident and happy.

He glanced at her. The serious concentration he'd focused on the tire morphed into something she couldn't name. "You're my good luck charm."

"No." She shook her head. "But I am your biggest fan."

CHAPTER ELEVEN

Early morning sunlight shone through the pine trees. Adam hurled a slider through the tire, then followed it up with a curveball. He'd been outside since dawn, throwing pitch after pitch. He hadn't slept well. Dreams of Gemma taunted him. He'd woken up aching, reaching for her, and more than disappointed when he'd realized she wasn't there to hold.

He trudged across the yard and collected balls, then returned to his throwing position. Confidence fired his muscles. Something had changed, he could feel it. But would that stay when he faced down a batter in a game?

Eight hours later, he stood on the pitcher's mound of the Trappers' baseball diamond. Three inches of snow covered the ground, but he imagined the sun shining, the stands filled with people, the pressures of a real game situation.

Connor stood at home plate, taking a few practice swings. Other members of the Trappers waited in the dugout, and the first and third basemen, along with an outfielder, took their respective positions on the field. His crew members were more than willing to step in and help. Somehow, he'd have to find a way to thank them.

Adam focused on the catcher. Every time his eyes landed on the catcher's mitt, he thought of Gemma and what she'd done for him. All other thoughts, all other worries, faded.

"Here's the wind-up, and the pitch..." One of the guys commentated from the bench.

Adam fired a fastball straight over home plate. It landed in the catcher's mitt.

"Strike!"

The grin spread across his face almost as fast as the pitch he'd thrown.

Gemma's cheer erupted from the dugout. Bear joined in with a bark. Having her there added a layer of comfort and a layer of tension. He wanted to do well for her, to show her how much he appreciated her help.

He turned his attention back to Connor. Two strikes later, he waited for another batter to step up to the plate. Pitch after pitch, strike after strike, he worked his way through the batters.

The tire hadn't magically changed his game.

Gemma had.

When she smiled at him, he felt his heart turn over in his chest. He wanted her with him. If he regained a spot in the majors, he wanted her by his side, needed her there. She was his good luck charm, his secret weapon, his everything. He needed to find out her plans for her career and if she would return to LA.

She and Bear walked onto the field after the game ended. The smile she'd worn for the entire evening widened. "You did great."

Unable to resist, he slid his arm around her waist and drew her into him. "I told you, you're my good luck charm."

"All I did was cheer you on." Pink flushed into her cheeks. "We should celebrate. How about a drink?"

The field lights flicked off. Darkness wrapped around them. His body craved hers. He didn't want to wake up without her in his bed again. "Sounds great. How about my place?"

The only light came from the overhead lights in the adjoining parking lot. Gemma bit her lip, but her body leaned into his. "I'll have to bring Bear with me."

"That's fine." He traced his finger down her cheek and tried to quell the aching need he had for her. "So what do you say? Come home with me?"

She studied him, her eyes swirling with nerves and needs. Finally, her breath released on a sigh and she pressed her cheek into his hand. "Let's go."

During the short ride home, she stayed close to his side, her warmth seeping through his clothes. Adam kept her hand tucked in his as they entered the darkened house. He'd been given a second chance with Gemma. Nothing was going to get in his way.

After the confusion of getting Bear settled, he returned to the living room.

"It's snowing." She placed her hands on the windowsill and gazed at the sky. She looked so *right* there, so perfect.

He crossed to her and wrapped his arms around her

waist. With a quiet sigh, she leaned against him. He rested his chin on her head. They watched the thick flakes swirling through the shadows.

Four years wasted. Four years that could have been filled with love and laughter. If he could turn back time, he'd do so many things differently.

"Have you thought about what you're going to do about Hollywood?" His fingers traced along her abdomen. Heat radiated through the soft flannel of his sleeve as he brushed her side.

"I love acting, but I don't want to live as a struggling actor anymore."

"What about living in LA?" He spoke casually, as if her answer wasn't weighing heavily on his mind and heart.

"If I don't have acting, then nothing's keeping me there."

His heartbeat ticked up a notch. She'd presented him with the perfect opportunity. "You don't belong on the other side of the country. You belong here with me. I want a second chance."

Turning in his arms, she faced him. Her mouth opened, then closed. Her eyes gazed into his for a long moment, then she inhaled a shaky breath. "For four years, I pretended to be fine and unaffected whenever anyone mentioned your name. But inside, I was dying. I'd lost you. And I hated myself for it."

"No." He cupped her face in his hands. "We lost each other."

A frown creased the smooth skin of her forehead. "What happens now? What about spring training? What about when you're on a team?"

"Come with me."

Her hands curled into his shirt, pulling him in closer. "But we're not the same people we were back then. What if we've both changed too much?" She bit her lip as she studied his face, her eyes wide and focused on his, her posture straight and body leaning into him.

He soothed her lip with the pad of his thumb. "I need you. That hasn't changed. I'm asking now what I should have asked you four years ago. Will you come with me?"

Tears glistened in her eyes, but she blinked them away. A wide smile spread across her face. Eyes sparkling, she nodded.

Warmth radiated out from his chest to his limbs. Things were going to be all right. He had his game back, thanks to his girl. His secret weapon would be with him every step of the way. But more importantly, he had her back in his life.

Sleek, toned arms wrapped around him so tight he had trouble breathing. "I'll follow you to whatever team picks you up, wherever it is."

With a groan, Adam crushed his mouth to hers and lifted her off her feet. Gratitude meshed with need. He'd take all night to show her how much she meant to him, how much her decision meant to him. Her lips opened under his and her hands slipped over his shoulders, holding on tight. He deepened the kiss, his lips demanding and coaxing, his tongue tasting and teasing. On her sigh, his arms tightened and locked her to him. Her body rubbed against his in a seductive swirl.

He swept his arm under her legs and carried her up the stairs. When they reached his bedroom, he set her on her feet and switched on a lamp next to the bed. Her gaze locked on his. Her smile, part sultry, part sweet, destroyed him.

In the dim light, he removed her shirt. His fingers brushed her newly exposed skin in a slow journey that stopped and explored every inch. On a soft moan, she leaned into his hands and he followed the path with his lips.

Her hands mimicked his movements. Breath backed up in his lungs. The feel of her hands on his skin drove him crazy.

He trailed his fingers over the sensitive skin from her wrist to her elbow. Her breath caught. Slowly, so slowly, he traced a path back to her palm. His thumb rubbed in a slow circle before he lifted her hand to his lips and pressed a kiss to its center.

"Adam." She directed his lips back to hers and wrapped herself around him. His blood pumped at the skin-on-skin contact of their torsos.

More.

Soft denim slipped down Gemma's legs, giving him a private striptease. Her purple lace bra and panties matched the color of her eyes.

She shivered.

"Cold?" He drew her against him. "I'll keep you warm."

She rose onto her toes, dragged his head down to hers, and paused, a breath away. "You always did take care of me." The lace scratched against his skin, creating an erotic friction.

"You're beautiful." He traced his fingertip over the swell of her breast. The softness of her skin was engrained in his memory, as was how perfectly she filled his hands. But the memory couldn't compare to the reality of touching her. She moaned when he stroked over the lace, and again when he stripped it away. Goosebumps pebbled on her skin when his hands closed over her again. He lowered his head to taste. With a sigh, she strained against his mouth, eyes fluttering closed. Steeped in her scent, he gave his attention to her other breast. "So beautiful."

"I could say the same about you. I love the way you look." She drew his face back to hers and nipped at his lower lip. Her fingers trailed a line down his abdomen. He sucked in a breath when she reached the waistband of his jeans. With a smile, she flicked open the button and took her time lowering his zipper. Her hand closed over him, and he lowered his forehead to hers, lost in her touch and the long strokes that shredded his control.

"Stop." Her hands felt amazing, but he needed to be inside her. Grasping her hands, Adam moved them to his shoulders and kicked out of his jeans. As soon as he was free, Gemma pulled him close again. Her eyes glowed with passion. She linked their fingers, and her lips sought his in a deep kiss that scrambled his thoughts.

He continued to kiss her as he backed up, still holding onto her hands, until he felt the bed against the backs of his legs. Trailing kisses across her face, he eased her onto the bed, and then covered her body with his.

Finally.

She was back in his bed, back in his life. And this time, she was staying.

Her hair fanned across his pillow, jet black on stark white. Just as he remembered. A small smile curved her lips. She traced her fingertips down his cheek and then rested them over his heart. She had to feel how quickly it beat.

He traced patterns on her skin and toyed with the lace riding low on her hip. Her breath caught when he slipped his fingers under the fabric and slid into her heat.

On a low moan, she shuddered and arched against his hand. Not enough. He drove her higher, until whimpers escaped her lips and she arched her hips. "More?"

She clawed at his shoulders. "Please."

"My pleasure." He drove another finger into her and slid over the spot that used to ignite her release.

"Adam." Her eyes locked with his and widened. She clenched and pulsed around his fingers in hot, wet waves. He kissed her until the storm quieted and her breathing returned to normal.

Then, she rolled to her side. "My turn." Her fingers teased his length and closed around him like a hot vise. Soft lips roamed his chest and stomach. When she ranged lower, his control snapped and he dragged her up. No more waiting. He tore the lace off her legs and removed his boxers.

Bracing over her, he paused, committing the moment to memory. Lips swollen from his kisses, cheeks flushed, Gemma held his gaze. Warmth swelled in his chest and his heart beat faster. He slid inside.

Her heat enveloped him and then she tightened around him and drove desire into a frenzied pace. Adam groaned and slammed his hips deep. Gemma's hands fisted in his hair and her hips urged him on.

Looking into the eyes of the only woman who'd ever mattered, he sought to give her every pleasure and rode out the wave of passion until she tightened around him. Her release flung him into the most intense burst of satisfaction he'd ever experienced. Adam claimed her lips as his heartbeat slowly returned to normal.

Gemma flowed into him until all his senses were full of her.

Joined together, he felt complete.

CHAPTER TWELVE

Gemma woke with Adam's arm wrapped around her waist and his warmth lined up against her body. She turned her head, and her lips grazed the underside of his jaw.

"Good morning." His mouth met hers in a kiss that swirled sensation from her head to her toes.

Soft whines and the sound of paws scratching at the door interrupted the quiet morning. She lifted her head. "Bear needs to go out."

"I'll take him and stay with him the entire time he's outside." His lips quirked, then he dropped a kiss on the corner of her mouth. "Be back in a few minutes. Don't go anywhere."

She laid against the pillows, snuggled in the big, soft bed, and listened to him talk to Bear as he headed down the hall. Unable to stop her smile, she stretched and then hugged his pillow to her chest. Even the sunlight pouring in the large windows shared her happy mood.

A few minutes later, footsteps padded down the hall, accompanied by a jangling collar. Bear trotted in at

Adam's side and settled on the floor at the foot of the bed. Adam held out her phone. "It chimed when I came back inside. I didn't want you to miss anything important."

She squinted at the screen. Several missed calls, plus a voicemail, plus a text from her agent.

As soon as you get this, call me ASAP.

Adam sat beside her. "Everything okay?"

Knowing he was thinking of his dad, she grasped his hand. "I'd better find out."

Liz answered on the first ring. "Great news. Lori MacDonald backed out of *Starlight*. She just found out she's three months pregnant and won't be able to complete the project or its sequel. They're filming both simultaneously. You were their next choice. So you're in. The part's yours."

"Are you serious?" Her heart beat like a drum. She squeezed Adam's hand. *Two* movies.

"I wouldn't be talking to you at four in the morning if I weren't."

Gemma glanced at the alarm clock on the bedside table and cringed. "I forgot about the time difference."

"Get yourself to the airport. I booked you on a flight leaving at eleven-thirty. You need to be in Seattle by this evening. You start shooting tomorrow."

"But wait, that's hardly any time."

"Things happen fast. I'll email you with all of the details." Liz ended the call.

"Oh my God." Energy filled her limbs. She dropped the phone and hurled herself into Adam's arms. "They gave me the role. The big role. Opposite Tyler Gregson." Clutching him tight, she blinked away the tears streaming down her face. "Finally. This is the chance I've been waiting for. And it happened two weeks before my deadline."

"I could hear everything she said." His hands rested on her back for a moment, then fell away.

A million details raced through her mind. "I have so much to do. Packing, printing out the boarding pass, calling my parents."

She pulled back. The high-flying exuberance crashed to a halt. Taking the role would take her away from Adam. Just the thought of being separated again formed a hole in her soul. How could she leave? "We need to talk."

Adam watched her with a carefully blank face. "Let me guess, you're not coming with me to spring training."

"I know I said I would, but…."

"But now you have a better offer." His mouth twisted into a grim smile.

"It's not like that." She grabbed his arm. "You know it's not."

"Isn't it?" He flicked a glance at her phone and stood. "Hollywood called and you answered."

"I can't turn down the role. This might be my last shot at making it. I've waited for so long. Someone finally wants me." Finally, she had her chance.

"*I* want you. I thought you wanted me, too." He exhaled a long, low breath and his hands squeezed into fists. "Was I the consolation prize?"

"How could you think of yourself that way?"

Tension tightened his features. "It's not too hard when you look at the situation from my angle. Maybe you only wanted me when things weren't going right for you."

"No. That's not—"

"Maybe you were settling for a second-best life with

me because that's all you thought you could get." He tensed and the muscles in his arms stood out.

"No. I swear—"

"But now that you have a chance at your career again, you're dropping me like I mean nothing, like *we* mean nothing, in favor of something better."

She shook her head and fought the wave of desperation rising in her chest. "That's not true. None of that's true. Acting was all I had for a long time. I've worked so hard for this opportunity. I have to see if I've got the chops, if I can cut it."

"I know you can cut it. You're damn good at what you do."

"All I want is a shot at my dream."

"Me, too." He turned and slammed his fist into the wall. "What happens if I get to spring training and my pitches are off again? You've been there for all of the good ones. What if you're the reason?"

"That's ridiculous. I'm not the reason. You're being superstitious." She dragged her hand through her hair. And then paused as a horrible idea planted itself in her mind. "Wait. Is that why you asked me to go with you—because you think I have some magic powers that control your pitches?"

His gaze darkened and his voice pitched low. "I want you with me regardless of your effect on my pitches."

But now that the idea had taken root shaking it free was impossible. "I wish I could believe you."

In three strides, he reached her, and caged her with his arms. "I don't lie."

She took in his glittering gaze, the harsh lines on his

face. He'd never been less than honest in the past. She desperately wanted to believe him. "Okay."

He pulled back and rubbed his hand over his face, then paced the length of the room. "How long will you be gone?"

"I'll be in Seattle three months, maybe a little longer."

"Maybe up to six if they're doing both movies. Where are you going after that?" With stiff movements, he pulled on jeans and a shirt.

Wrapping the sheet around her, she searched for her clothes. It was too soon to know how the movie would go, how her life would be affected. "Back to LA, I guess."

"Back to LA." Mouth firm, jaw as set as stone, he lifted his brow. "For how long?"

"I don't know." She couldn't afford to jet all around the country, catching flights back and forth from LA to wherever he ended up. She needed to save as much money as possible and be available for her agent and for auditions. The last four years had shown her one thing, she had to rely on herself.

"For good?" His body stilled, his focus clear and direct on her face, as he waited for her answer.

Saying yes would mean heartache, but saying no could be a lie. "We can make this work."

"How? By you flying in for an afternoon a few times a year? By me swinging by for a night or a weekend when I'm in town on a road trip?" A vein in his neck pulsed.

Sickness coated her stomach, like something vital was slipping through her fingers and she couldn't grasp hold. "I want more than that. I want us to be together."

"Pretty damn hard to be together when we're living on

opposite sides of the country. I don't want to have to fly for six hours every damn time I want to see you."

"Neither do I, but what am I supposed to do, ask you to skip out on baseball and your family and move to LA? Or, would you ask me to give up my dream?" She'd worked too hard, she'd fought too long. He had, too.

His fist slammed onto the top of the bedpost. "No, but I want to see you every day, and I want you lying next to me every night."

"Don't you think I want that, too?" She wanted him as much as he claimed he wanted her.

He sat on the edge of the bed and rubbed his hands over his face. "I don't know anymore. Maybe you exaggerated your feelings for me because it suited you at the time."

"You really think I can fake my emotions that way?"

His brown eyes pinned her with a heated stare. She could almost feel the flames. "You're a damn fine actress. Would it really be a stretch?"

She gasped and put her hand on her stomach. If he'd hit her, it would have hurt less. "If that's the way you feel, it's probably best that I'm leaving now."

"I'll drive you to my sister's." He strode to the bedroom door. Bear barked and padded to his side. Adam turned back, his hand on the dog's head. "What are you going to do with Bear while you're in Seattle?"

Her mind spun. She took a deep breath and grasped for a rational thought. "My vet's office has a small boarding section but I don't have time to go to LA first. Maybe—"

"You can't leave him with the vet for months. His separation anxiety will skyrocket. I'll keep him."

"You can't keep him." She motioned for Bear and wrapped both arms around him.

"He's familiar with me. It's the best choice for him."

Swiping away her tears, she stared at Adam's hard expression. Bear would be happier with Adam, but...she couldn't let him go, that was too much. Too much responsibility for Adam and too much loss for her to handle. She couldn't lose them both.

"I just can't give him up. I love him."

A pained expression shot across his face, then disappeared. "I'll get him to you once you're back in LA."

He didn't say he'd be the one to deliver the dog.

If he told her he loved her, she would have done anything for him. But he hadn't said the words. Neither had she, and with the awful words they'd just hurled at each other, it was probably best left unsaid. Words were being turned around and twisted. No way should a declaration of love ever be used as a weapon.

Thinking of a life without Adam gutted her. Suddenly cold, she wrapped her arms around her body. The alarm clock ticked away another precious minute.

"So this is it." She wasn't ready to say goodbye. Tears clogged her throat. She pulled on her jeans and reached for the dog.

Life wasn't fair.

Why did the realization of one dream have to result in the destruction of another?

When she looked up, Adam was gone.

She couldn't shake the feeling that once she left, she'd never see him again.

CHAPTER THIRTEEN

After dropping Gemma off at his sister's house, Adam took off into the woods with Bear. The rushed morning repeated in his head. A sexy reunion ending in a screeching halt of a breakup. So much worse than the first time around.

A couple walked hand-in-hand along the trail in front of him. Too much like Gemma and him. All thoughts of clearing his mind evaporated. He trekked back to his house.

An hour later, he strode into the office. Bear trotted by his side. His father's car was in the parking lot. Thankfully, Jocelyn's wasn't. After seeing her expression that morning when Gemma exited his truck, he could only imagine what his sister would have to say.

His father looked up from his desk. "That dog is huge."

Adam grunted in agreement and poured a cup of coffee as black as his mood, then sat behind his desk. Bear settled on the floor at his feet. He hadn't left Adam's side since they'd driven away from Gemma.

"Where's Gemma?"

"On her way to Seattle. She got a movie role."

"Good for her. Jocelyn told me about her troubles there."

Adam grunted again and reached for a pen. He'd bury himself in work until he stopped thinking about her.

"You don't sound very happy."

He tossed his pen down. "I am happy for her. Why is everyone so chatty today?"

His father raised a brow, then pushed away from the desk and walked to the window. "You've done a lot of good for this company since you took over."

He nodded and swallowed a mouthful of coffee. Bitter and cold. He grimaced and set the cup on his desk. "I did the best I could."

"You kept everything running smoothly. I didn't have to worry about a thing."

Adam leaned back in his chair. He studied his father for signs of fatigue or sickness. "You feeling okay?"

"I'm feeling fine. Do I have to be sick or in a hospital bed to tell you I'm proud of you?"

"I did what any son would do."

"No, you didn't. Not every son would give up his dream for his old man."

"It wasn't hard to give up when I couldn't pitch worth a damn."

"You can now. I saw you the other day, pitching balls to the Trappers. You have your swagger again. You're ready to get back to baseball." With a nod, he turned toward the coffee pot.

Adam picked up the baseball he'd brought in to keep Bear entertained. Without Gemma by his side, would he be a success? "Whether I'll carry it out to the mound in a real game is still up in the air."

"You will. I have no doubt. Neither did Gemma. She cares about you."

He couldn't stop the low growl emitting from his throat. "We need to talk about the business. If I'm going back to baseball, we need someone here to take my place. I think Connor would do a good job. He cares about this company as much as we do."

"No one could take your place." His dad clapped his hand on Adam's shoulder in a brief pat. "But I agree with Connor taking on more work. He has a good head on his shoulders, and he's content to work here throughout the year. I'll hire some more help to ease his schedule once baseball season begins."

The door burst open and crashed into the wall. Bear jumped to his feet, placed himself in front of Adam, and tensed, ready to attack.

"You idiot. She loves you." Jocelyn stormed into the room and straight to Adam's desk. Eyes shooting daggers, she slammed her hands down on the surface. Coffee sloshed over the rim of his cup. "She *loves* you. And you let her go."

"Stay out of it." The snarled warning would have been enough for most people to heed, but not his sister.

"How could you let her go? You're so perfect for each other."

His muscles tightened. "This isn't your fight."

"You should have gone with her. If you loved her, you'd find a way to make it work." She turned to their father. "Don't you agree?"

Dad rubbed his hands over his face and sighed.

"When your mom died, I felt like a piece of me died with her. I've missed her every day for the past fifteen years."

Adam shook his head. What was Jocelyn doing? They were supposed to keep him stress-free, not make him upset thinking about their mother. "Dad, you don't have to talk about this."

"I want to. It's important. If you're lucky enough to find someone who makes you feel complete, you should fight like hell to keep them." Pinning Adam with a stare, he walked back to his desk. "All I want is for both of you to be happy."

Adam glared at the spot of spilled coffee surrounding his cup. Happy. That was all he wanted, too. He'd ruined his chances when he'd lashed out at Gemma, all because he was afraid of losing her. But short of cloning himself or making time stand still, how could he solve the problem of distance and mismatched schedules?

Bear padded to his side and rested his snout on Adam's knee. The dog's sad eyes were likely a reflection of his own. His rubbed his hand over the fur head. He and Gemma had promised to take care of Bear, and each other, all those years ago. He didn't want anyone else but her by his side.

His phone signaled a text message alert. Adam yanked it out of his pocket. Not from Gemma. Disappointment hitched onto annoyance. He didn't want to spend his life holding his breath, waiting for her next text or phone call, or going months without touching her. He wanted her, in the flesh, with him every day.

He read the text.

Dom: Leaving for Arizona soon. Call me when you

know where you're playing. Let me know if you need anything or if I can do anything.

His hand hovered over the keys. He needed Gemma. Dom couldn't help with that.

Setting the phone aside, he opened his desk drawer. The retirement papers, wrinkled from her hands, lay on top of the jumbled mess of office supplies.

She'd gone out of her way to help him fix his game.

Giving up Bear was too much for her because she loved the animal. But did she love him? She'd said she'd wanted to be together. Despite what he'd said to her, he knew she hadn't faked her emotions.

He loved her. That was the bottom line. She completed him. She made him whole.

The solution came to him, crystal clear. He grabbed his phone and typed a rapid response to Dom. Adrenaline coursed through his system. He pushed to his feet. His chair shot out and hit the wall behind him, startling Bear.

Jocelyn stared at him as he moved closer to her desk. "What's wrong?"

"I'm calling in the favor you owe me."

Her eyes narrowed, and she crossed her arms over her chest. "Bring it on."

"I'm not sure when I'll be back, maybe a few days, maybe a week. Cover for me while I'm gone. And take care of Bear. That means keeping him with you at all times."

"Where are you going?"

"Dad's right. I can't lose Gemma." He grabbed his coat off the hook and strode out of the building.

The game of his life was on the line. It was up to him to make the save.

Adjusting the strap on his travel bag, Adam exited the elevator and then strode down the hotel's quiet hall. In the three days since his text to Dom, his world had been a whirlwind of travel, calls with his agent, more texts with Dom, and finally a meeting with the Riptide's GM.

Frenetic energy buzzed through his system. One hurdle had been cleared, but he still had more to go if he had any hope of fixing his future.

He knocked on the hotel room door. Moments later, it opened and Dom Torres filled the doorway. His friend grinned and then grabbed Adam in a tight hug. "Dude, it's so good to see you."

Happiness poked through his worries like sunshine beaming through clouds. A familiar and friendly face was exactly what Adam needed. He returned the hug, too overwhelmed to speak for a moment. Clasping Dom hard, he fought for control. "You too."

Dom lowered his arms, stepped back, and waved him into the room. "Come in."

He dropped his bag close to a few suitcases stacked next to an armchair and scanned the large room.

A long, lanky man with a buzz cut sprawled across the bed closest to the door. "Hey, I'm Slade."

He shook the Riptide first baseman's hand. Dom had mentioned in their text exchange that he was sharing the suite with his teammate who was like an honorary younger brother. Adam looked forward to getting to know him. "It's good to meet you."

Dom sat on the other bed amid the clutter of two books, a tablet, a phone, and a bottle of orange sports drink. He gestured for Adam to sit on the long couch that lined the wall under the window. "So, how was the meeting with the GM?"

"My tryout is tomorrow."

Grinning, Dom pumped his fist in the air. "Yes! It's going to be so good having you on the team."

"*If* I make the team."

"You will."

He wiped damp palms over his jeans. "I don't know, man. I hope so."

"You *will*," Dom said again. His gaze zeroed in on the spot where the ball had crashed into Adam's skull. Then he quickly dropped his focus to the couch. "Housekeeping has assured me that couch converts into a very comfortable bed."

Adam resisted the urge to touch his head when Dom's gaze flashed to the spot once again. "I appreciate you not minding that I crash here tonight."

Slade lifted a shoulder and smiled. "The more the merrier."

"It's the least I can do." Regret and remorse laced through Dom's words and his expression. He glanced at the spot one more time.

Enough.

"This," Adam pointed to his head, "wasn't your fault. A freak accident is a freak accident. You weren't aiming for me. I get feeling bad or guilty, okay? I do. I've been there feeling those same things when I've hit a batter with a ball and it ended up causing a broken bone or something else that knocked the guy out of the lineup. But I'm fine. Completely fine."

A single brow rose as Dom studied Adam's face. "Are

you really? Not just physically, but mentally and emotionally?"

"It took a lot of work and a lot of help from people, but yeah." Thoughts immediately flew to Gemma. He'd do whatever it took to show her how much she had helped him. Making the team would be a damn fine start.

The creases of concern around Dom's eyes eased. "I'm happy to hear that. Still, I don't know if I'll ever be able to look at you and *not* think about what happened."

Adam nodded, understanding his friend's statement. Knowing that one's actions, however unintentional, had caused someone else suffering was a tough thing to get past. Hopefully, he'd make the team and then he and Dom could create so many good memories that the lone bad one would be long forgotten. "Well, when you find yourself thinking about it, you better also remember how much you were there for me with texts and calls throughout my recovery. You helped me a lot."

Slade sat up and grabbed a bottle of water off of the bedside table. His gaze darted between Dom and Adam, and then he smiled and his eyes sparked with mischief. "Dom, if you want to help him out some more, you could give Adam your bed and take the convertible couch tonight."

"Done."

Laughing, Adam shook his head. "You're too tall, your legs would hang off the edge. The couch is fine with me. "

"No. Slade's right." Dom finally smiled. "I want you on this team, so whatever I can do to make that happen..."

"You can keep your bed. But you could watch old game footage with me tonight and help me get a feel for the guys I might be pitching against tomorrow."

Dom grabbed his tablet. "Great idea. Let's get started right now."

Slade stood and stretched and then helped Dom clear the rest of the clutter from his bed. "I'll help you too. Don't worry about anything, Adam. We've got you."

The support and friendship meant more than words could say. Filled with gratitude, Adam joined them as the familiar sounds of balls cracking off bats emanated from the tablet. "I appreciate it, guys. I have a lot riding on this tryout."

More than a lot.

More like everything.

CHAPTER FOURTEEN

One week after she'd said goodbye to Adam, Gemma sat in her trailer, on the set of *Starlight*, studying her lines. Her experience so far had been an actor's dream. The cast had good chemistry with each other and had welcomed her with open arms. The writing was witty and compelling, and there was enough action and romance in the plot to satisfy most viewers. All signs pointed to her career skyrocketing. Finally, she had everything she wanted.

And she was miserable.

She glanced at the page. She'd been staring at the same two lines for over an hour. Rain pounded on the roof in persistent taps. The tiny window over her shoulder gave her a glimpse of gray skies. The same gray as the day she watched Adam pitch balls to the Trappers. Filming had stopped for two days because of the weather. Some of the crew had invited her to tour the city, but she'd begged off, feigning exhaustion. Only, it wasn't so feigned. Emotionally, she was a wreck.

If she'd made the right choice, why did it hurt so much?

She missed Adam and Bear.

Tears filled her eyes, blurring the words. They spilled over and splotched onto the page. Her stomach ached, her head hurt, she was tired of crying, tired of checking her phone to see if he called, and tired of being disappointed that he hadn't.

She couldn't blame him. They'd said all there was to say. Except *I love you*. Neither of them had said that. But she did love him, and loving him meant wanting what was best for him, and what was best for him was baseball.

What was best for her was…him.

Nothing made sense without him. She couldn't lose him again. There had to be a way to make their situation work. If he earned a spot on a big league roster, she'd go anywhere he did. She'd find a way to fit acting and Hollywood into her life with him. As long as she had Adam, everything else would fall into place. It had to.

Tossing the script aside, she stood, then grabbed her jacket and purse. She needed to be with him, to feel his arms around her, to tell him that being together was all that mattered. They'd find a solution. This time, they'd discuss it like rational adults, and in the absence of wild emotions, they'd figure out a way to fulfill both their needs.

If she caught the next flight out, she'd arrive in Hunter's Peak by midnight. They could spend the weekend together and she'd arrive back on the set in time for her five a.m. call on Monday morning.

If he'd still have her.

She paused. What if he didn't want—

No. He had to listen. She couldn't be too late.

She rushed out of the trailer. Drizzling rain spritzed her face. Ducking her head down, she increased her pace toward the parking lot. Raised voices carried in from her left. She glanced over to the security station and skidded to a stop.

Adam stood toe to toe with the head of security. The burly guard crossed his arms over his chest. "Look, pal, you can't come on set without a pass."

"Call her," Adam growled, his hair disheveled, clothes wrinkled and shadows under his eyes.

Flutters with the strength of a thousand butterflies danced in her stomach. On jittery limbs, Gemma broke into a run. "Adam."

Both men looked over at her. Adam's scowl faded, and he stared at her with the most intense expression she'd ever seen. He dropped his duffel bag and strode toward her. She threw herself into his arms and held on tight. Her fingers curled into the back of his jacket.

His arms banded around her and his fingers tangled in her hair. His familiar scent brought tears to her eyes and a lump in a throat. She clasped him as hard as she could, and it still wasn't enough.

With a gentle tug on her hair, he angled her head back and then his lips descended and covered hers. Warm, firm, and real.

She opened for him and poured her feelings into the kiss.

The security guard cleared his throat. "I guess you know this guy."

She broke the kiss and smiled into Adam's eyes. "He's a friend of mine."

"I hope I'm more than that." He raised a brow at the

guard, who stepped aside and allowed him entrance, then picked up his bag. "We need to talk."

"My trailer is close." She kept her voice as even as possible so she wouldn't break down. By the time they reached the trailer, the rain had soaked their clothes and hair. Handing him a towel, she used another to squeeze water out of her hair.

His gaze wandered over the small space. "How do you like filming?"

"The role is perfect for me and the cast is amazing."

"You're happy?" He stood, posture straight, perfectly still, and waited for her answer.

She couldn't answer the question without her throat thickening with tears. Arms crossed over her chest, she leaned against her chair. "Why are you here?"

"Bear misses you."

Her chin quivered. She shook her head to hold her tears at bay. "I miss him, too."

"More than that, I'm here because I wasn't happy."

She moved to his side. "Oh, Adam."

"Wait. Hear me out." He held up his hand. "Please."

"All right." Gripping the towel, she waited.

He raked his fingers through his hair. "I need to apologize. The things I said to you were awful."

"We both said things we regretted." She tossed the towel onto a chair and laid her hand on his arm.

His hand covered hers, competent, strong, and warm. He laced their fingers together. "Connor's taking over my place in my dad's company. My dad will stay on as a consultant, but Connor will handle the everyday details."

"That's great. He's a good guy." If he'd settled his

obligation at the company, then... She tightened her hold on his hand. "Does that mean what I think it means?"

He nodded. "You're looking at the number four starting pitcher for the Los Angeles Riptide."

Elation surged and propelled her off her feet. With a shriek, she grabbed him in a hug. "Congratulations, that's amazing."

"I'm glad you think so." His arms came around her and locked at her back.

His words fully sunk in. She leaned back to study his face. "Los Angeles? But what happened to the East Coast teams?"

"They weren't where you are. I met with the Riptide's managing staff and convinced them to give me a shot." A muscle jumped in his jaw. "I found a house in Glendale. I think you'd like it, and there's a yard for Bear. Glendale is an easy drive from LA."

Hot tears gathered at the corner of her eyes. "You did this for me."

"I did it for us. I love you."

Her heart swelled to bursting. "I love you, too."

His eyes closed for a moment and his arms tightened their hold.

She cupped his cheek and searched his face. "You'll be happy there?"

"As long as I'm with you, I'm happy."

"Are you sure? Because I don't have to live in LA to be an actor. All I want is to be with you."

"There's no reason we both can't have our dreams." Adam reached into his pocket and drew out a ring. Two diamond hearts, linked together, on a platinum band.

For a moment, time seemed to stand still. For a moment, she forgot to breathe.

He clasped her hand. "I was an idiot to lose you the first time. I won't lose you again. Marry me. Let's make a life together."

She nodded, and he slipped the ring on her finger. The gems gleamed and sparkled in the lights. She slid her hands up into his hair and brought his mouth down to hers. "With you, here, now, I have everything I ever wanted."

EPILOGUE

Eight months later…

Bright sunlight glittered on the waves of the Pacific and baked the sunbathers lying on colorful towels. Gulls screech overhead. Gemma raised her gaze to the clear sky and watched them soar. She wiggled her toes in the warm sand and turned toward Adam. "I love it out here."

"Ready?" He reached out his hand, and the sunlight flashed off his wedding band. A thrill zipped through her when she slipped her hand in his. Like her ring, a perfect fit.

"Ready." They waded into the ocean. Cool, refreshing waves crashed around them. She skimmed her fingers through the water and jumped the incoming swell. "I'm glad we took the day off to play. I needed a break from packing and studying my script."

Next week, they'd head to Canada to begin her next project. By choosing roles that would be filmed in the off-season, she'd been able to follow Adam on the road during baseball season. Spending time together mattered more than anything else. Nothing was better than falling asleep in his arms, or waking the same way, or the thousands of other, special moments that made up sharing their lives.

"You've been working hard. I'm so proud of you." He linked their fingers together and brought them to his lips. "Two movies filmed and three more projects lined up. You're on fire."

Bear ran along the sand and then charged into the water, splashing a course straight toward them. Adam turned her in his arms, protecting her from the force of the dog's greeting. He took the baseball out of Bear's mouth and hurled it toward the shore. With an excited bark, the black and white bundle of fur took off after his treasure.

Gemma pressed close to Adam and brushed her lips over his cheek. "Not to be outdone by you, Mr. Comeback Player of the Year."

He grinned. Although he downplayed his achievement, she was still riding high from the previous evening's major league award ceremony. He deserved the accolades. No player worked harder than him. "I love being part of the Riptide. I owe Dom for helping me get a meeting with the front office."

"You thanked him when you received your award. His grin was so wide, I thought his face would split."

"And when you grabbed him in a hug, I was sure it would." Adam nudged her shoulder.

"Hey, I was excited." She stretched and sighed and stared at the vast expanse of ocean and shore. "I know you like the beach, but are you sure you didn't want to celebrate in another way?"

"Any excuse to see you in a bikini works for me. Besides, it reminds me of the first time we met."

"Only it's a lot warmer now." The heat felt good against her skin. And even better when she snuggled closer to Adam. Frigid lake or warm beach, anywhere with him was perfect.

His hands slid in a slow path from her shoulders to her wrists. "You're an actress. You could pretend you're cold and let me warm you up."

She grinned. "I'm f-f-freezing. Can't you tell?"

Strong arms wrapped around her waist. He dipped his head, and his lips hovered an inch from hers. "I love you."

"I love you, too." She closed the distance. Happiness bubbled up and overflowed, leaving her giddy. Nothing felt better than being in his arms and tasting his kiss.

Adam's fingers traced a pattern on her back. He lifted his head, and his dark brown eyes grew serious. "I know I told the world last night, but I need to say it again now, here, with just the two of us. Thank you."

"I didn't do anything."

"Everyone wrote me off—the coaches, the media, myself. But you didn't. You believed in me. You inspire me, every day. None of this would have happened without you. You'll always be my MVP."

Her heart swelled, and she blinked to quell the tears threatening to form. "Last night, the league's most valuable player received a trophy."

A grin spread across his face. "Want one?"

She shook her head. "As long as I have you by my side, I have everything I need."

"I'll always be there. No matter what life pitches to us, we'll face it together."

"I like those odds." She tilted her head to accept his kiss.

Thank you so much for reading *Rekindled*! I would appreciate it if you would help others enjoy this book too! Please recommend to others and leave a review. Reviews, even one line long, help other readers discover authors' books.

Don't miss the other books in the Game of Love series:

Captivated

Domingo Torres, star center fielder for the Los Angeles Riptide, needs to stay off management's radar after a Spring Training game ended in flying fists and bloodshed. He's ordered to keep a lid on his temper and a low profile for the rest of the season. Keeping his focus solely on baseball isn't a problem — until he meets his sexy new neighbor, and his thoughts shift to a lot more than his batting average.

After years of complete control in handling every aspect of her brother's multi-platinum selling rock band, Irisa Rostov is ready to crack. And it doesn't help that the band is on the verge of self-destruction. Playing peacemaker and keeping them together for the last eight weeks of their spring concert series is all that matters, until she meets Dom, and the feelings he stirs up causes the guards around her heart to weaken.

Getting distracted by romance is the last thing Irisa wants, and being in the headlines is the last thing Dom needs, but their attraction is undeniable, their connection is immediate, and staying away is impossible.

Enamored

A baseball romance double-header! Two stories in one!

After a Spring Training stunt saddles Liam York with a broken ankle, the *League's Best Mascot* is forced to share the spotlight with the team's solution: a temporary friend for Fin the Shark. But his new co-worker tests the limits of his control.

Claire Devereux spent years caring for her siblings and is more than ready for some fun. She loves every aspect of being Fin's new friend Fiona and is determined to make the temporary gig permanent.

As romance blooms between their on-field personalities, Liam and Claire give in to their passion off the field too. But curve balls from every direction test whether they're better as a duo or if it's every mascot for him/herself.

Meanwhile…

First baseman Slade MacInnes has a lot of balls in the air. His contract is expiring, he's just found his birth parents, and his agreement to do some work with a children's charity has led him to the very sexy and sweet Savanna Soto.

Savanna works hard granting wishes to kids with life-threatening illnesses, something her sister never lived to experience. Slade's no-fear attitude and adrenaline-junkie adventures make her want to break out of her self-imposed safety bubble and *live*.

Slade figures he's just the man to help her conquer her fears. Each activity draws them closer together with an attraction that sizzles. But when life pushes their differences to a head, will fear win out or can love save the game?

Check out the series:
    https://www.susanscottshelley.com/gameoflove

ABOUT THE AUTHOR

USA TODAY bestselling author Susan Scott Shelley writes romance with heat and heart that celebrates love without limits. She enjoys watching hockey, training for her next run, reading romance novels, and binging episodes of her favorite British TV shows. Susan lives in Philadelphia with her husband and also works as a professional voice over artist. A city girl who likes being out in nature as often as possible, she has yet to meet a plant she hasn't wanted to take home and she really wants a pet crow.

Visit her at https://susanscottsshelley.com.

ALSO BY SUSAN SCOTT SHELLEY

Love & Rugby, vol. 1, Love & Rugby, vol. 2,
Love & Rugby, the Complete Collection

Love & Rugby: Season of Love
Savor, Seduce, Stay
Love & Rugby: Season of Love, the Complete Collection

Buffalo Bedlam series
Making His Move, Fighting For More, Taking His Shot
Playing to Win (series collection)

Rocked by Love series
Love Notes, Love Song

Game of Love series
Rekindled, Captivated, Enamored
Game of Love (series collection)

Holiday Hearts series
Kiss Me Again, More Than Words, All I Want, Marry Me
Holiday Hearts (series collection)

Other Novellas
Flirting on Ice, Simmering Ice, Tackled by the Girl Next Door

Sign up for Susan's newsletter:
https://susanscottshelley.com/newsletter

www.ingramcontent.com/pod-product-compliance
Lightning Source LLC
Chambersburg PA
CBHW070604180626
46817CB00005B/1992